WHY WE BROKE UP

WHY WE BROKE UP

NOVEL BY
DANIEL HANDLER

ART BY
MAIRA KALMAN

LITTLE, BROWN AND COMPANY
NEW YORK   BOSTON

Text copyright © 2011 by Daniel Handler / Art copyright © 2011 by Maira Kalman

Little, Brown and Company

Hachette Book Group / 1290 Avenue of the Americas, New York, NY 10104
Visit our website at www.lb-teens.com

Little, Brown and Company is a division of Hachette Book Group, Inc.
The Little, Brown name and logo are trademarks of Hachette Book Group, Inc.

The publisher is not responsible for websites (or their content) that are not owned by the publisher.

First Paperback Edition: December 2013
First published in hardcover in December 2011 by Little, Brown and Company

Library of Congress Cataloging-in-Publication Data

Handler, Daniel.
Why we broke up / Daniel Handler ; art by Maira Kalman. — 1st ed.
p. cm.
Summary: Sixteen-year-old Min Green writes a letter to Ed Slaterton in which she
breaks up with him, documenting their relationship and how items in the accompanying box,
from bottle caps to a cookbook, foretell the end.
ISBN 978-0-316-12725-7 (hc) / ISBN 978-0-316-12726-4 (pb)
[1. Dating (Social customs)—Fiction. 2. Souvenirs (Keepsakes)—Fiction. 3. Letters—Fiction.]
I. Kalman, Maira, ill. II. Title.
PZ7.H1925Why 2012
[Fic]—dc22
2011009714

10 9 8 7 6 5 4

APS

Printed in China

For Charlotte—
why we got together

—D.H. + M.K.

Dear Ed,

In a sec you'll hear a thunk. At your front door, the one nobody uses. It'll rattle the hinges a bit when it lands, because it's so weighty and important, a little jangle along with the thunk, and Joan will look up from whatever she's cooking. She will look down in her saucepan, worried that if she goes to see what it is it'll boil over. I can see her frown in the reflection of the bubbly sauce or whatnot. But she'll go, she'll go and see. You won't, Ed. You wouldn't. You're upstairs probably, sweaty and alone. You should be taking a shower, but you're heartbroken on the bed, I hope, so it's your sister, Joan, who will open the door even though the thunk's for you. You won't even know or hear what's being dumped at your door. You won't even know why it even happened.

It's a beautiful day, sunny and whatnot. The sort of day when you think everything will be all right, etc. Not the right day for this, not for us, who went out when it rains, from October 5 until November 12. But it's December now, and the sky is bright, and it's clear to me. I'm telling you why we broke up, Ed. I'm writing it in this letter, the whole truth of why it happened. And the truth is that I goddamn loved you so much.

The thunk is the box, Ed. This is what I am leaving you. I found it down in the basement, just grabbed the box when all of our things were too much for my bed stand drawer. Plus I thought my mom would find some of the things, because she's a snoop for my secrets. So it all went into the box and the box went into my closet with some shoes on top of it I never wear. Every last souvenir of the love we had, the prizes and the debris of this relationship, like the glitter in the gutter when the parade has passed, all the everything and whatnot kicked to the curb. I'm dumping the whole box back into your life, Ed, every item of you and me. I'm dumping this box on your porch, Ed, but it is you, Ed, who is getting dumped.

The thunk, I admit it, will make me smile. A rare thing lately. Lately I've been like Aimeé Rondelé in *The Sky Cries Too*, a movie, French, you haven't seen. She plays an assassin and dress designer, and she only smiles twice in the whole film. Once is when the kingpin who killed her father gets thrown off the building, which is not the time I'm thinking of. It's the time at the end, when she finally has the envelope with the photographs and burns it unopened in the gorgeous ashtray and she knows it's over and lights a cigarette and stands in that perfect green of a dress watching the blackbirds swarm and flurry around the church spire. I can see it. The world is right again, is the smile. I loved you and now here's back your stuff, out of my life like you belong, is the smile. I know you can't see it, not you, Ed, but maybe if I tell you the whole plot you'll understand it this once, because even now I want you to see it. I don't love you anymore, of course I don't, but still there's something I can show you. You know I want to be a director, but you could never truly see the movies in my head and that, Ed, is why we broke up.

I wrote my favorite quote on the lid of this box, from Hawk Davies, who is a legend, and I'm writing this letter with the lid of this box as a desk so I can feel Hawk Davies flowing through every word I write to you. Al's father's shop's truck rattles so sometimes the words are shaky, so that's your tough luck as you read every word of this. I called Al this morning, and right away when I said, "Guess what?" he said, "You're going to ask me to help you run an errand in my dad's truck."

"You're good at guessing," I said. "That's very close."

"Close?"

"OK, yes, that's it."

"OK, give me a sec to find my keys and I'll pick you up."

"They should be in your jacket, from last night."

"You're good too."

"Don't you want to know what the errand is?"

"You can tell me when I get there."

"I want to tell you now."

"It doesn't matter, Min," he said.

"Call me La Desperada," I said.

"What?"

"I'm giving back Ed's stuff." I said it after a deep breath, and then I heard him take one, too.

"Finally."

"Yeah. My end of the deal, right?"

"When you're ready, yeah. So, you're ready?"

Another one, deeper but shakier. "Yes."

"Are you sad about it?"

"No."

"Min."

"OK, yes."

"OK, I have my keys. Five minutes."

"OK."

"OK?"

"It's just that I'm looking at the quote on the box. You know, Hawk Davies. You either have the feeling or you don't."

"Five minutes, Min."

"Al, I'm sorry. I shouldn't have even—"

"Min, it's OK."

"You don't have to. It's just that the box is so heavy I don't know—"

"It's *OK*, Min. And of course I have to."

"Why?"

He sighed through the phone and I kept staring at the top of the box. I'll miss seeing the quote when I open my closet, but I will not, Ed, I don't miss you. "Because, Min," Al said, "the keys were right in my jacket, where you said they'd be."

Al is a good, good person, Ed. It was Al's party where you and I first met, not that he invited you because he had no opinion of you then and so didn't invite you or any of your grunty jock crowd to his Bitter Sixteen party. I left school early to help him with the dandelion green pesto made with gorgonzola cheese instead of parmesan for extra bitterness that we served on top of the squid ink gnocchi from his dad's shop and mix up the blood orange vinaigrette for the fruit salad and cook up that huge 89 percent cacao dark chocolate cake in the shape of a big black heart so bitter we couldn't really eat it, but you just waltzed in un-invited with Trevor and Christian and all them to skulk in the corner and not touch anything except, like, nine bottles of Scarpia's Bitter Black Ale. I was a good guest, Ed, and you didn't even say "bitter birthday" to your host and give a present, and that is why we broke up.

These are the caps from the bottles of Scarpia's Bitter Black Ale that you and I drank in Al's backyard that night. I can see the stars bright and prickly and our breathing steamy in the cold, you in your team jacket and me in that cardigan of Al's I always borrow at his house. He had it waiting, clean and folded, when I went upstairs with him to give him his present before the guests arrived.

"I told you I didn't want a present," Al said. "The party was enough I told you, without the obligatory—"

"It's not *obligatory*," I said, having used the same vocabulary flash cards with Al when we were freshmen. "I found something. It's perfect. Open it."

He took the bag from me, nervous.

"Come on, happy birthday."

"What is it?"

"Your heart's desire. I hope. Open it. You're driving me crazy."

Rustle rustle rip, and he sort of gasped. It was very satisfying. "Where did you find this?"

"Does it not," I said, "I mean *exactly*, look like what the guy wears in the party scene in *Una settimana straordinaria*?"

He smiled into the slender box. It was a necktie, dark green with modern diamond shapes stitched into it in a line. It'd been in my sock drawer for months, waiting. "Take it out," I said. "Wear it tonight. Does it not, *exactly*?"

"When he gets out of the Porcini XL10," he said, but he was looking at me.

"Your absolute favorite scene in any movie. I hope you love it."

"I do, Min. I do love it. Where did you find it?"

"I snuck off to Italy and seduced Carlo Ronzi, and when he fell asleep I slipped into his costume archives—"

"Min."

"Tag sale. Let me put it on you."

"I can tie my own tie, Min."

"Not on your birthday." I fiddled with his collar. "They're going to eat you up in this."

"Who is?"

"Girls. Women. At the party."

"Min, it's going to be the same friends who always come."

"Don't be so sure."

"Min."

"Aren't you ready? I mean, I am. Totally over Joe. That make-out date in the summer, no way. And you. LA was like a million years—"

"It was last year. *This* year, really, but last school year."

"Yeah, and junior year's started up, the first big thing we're having. Aren't you ready? For a party and romance and *Una settimana straordinaria*? Aren't you, I don't know, hungry for—"

"I'm hungry for the pesto."

"Al."

"And for people to have fun. That's it. It's just a birthday."

"It's Bitter Sixteen! You're telling me that if the girl pulled up in the Porcini whatever—"

"OK, yes, the car I'm ready for."

"When you're twenty-one," I told him, "I'll buy you the car. Tonight it's the tie, and something—"

He sighed, so slow, at me. "You can't do this, Min."

"I can find you your heart's desire. Look, I did it once."

"It's the tie you can't do. It's like you're braiding a lanyard. Let go."

"OK, OK."

"But thank you."

I fixed his hair. "Happy birthday," I said.

"The cardigan's over there when you get cold."

"Yes, because I'll be huddled outside somewhere and you'll be in a world of passion and adventure."

"And pesto, Min. Don't forget about the pesto."

Downstairs Jordan had put on the bitter mix we'd slaved over, and Lauren was walking around with a long wooden match lighting candles. *Quiet on the set*, is how it felt, just ten minutes with everything crackling in the air and nothing happening. And then with a swoosh of his parents' screen door, a carload of Monica and her brother and that guy who plays tennis came in with wine they'd snitched from her mom's housewarming—still wrapped in silly gift paper—and turned up the music and the night began to begin. I kept quiet about my quest but kept looking for someone for Al. But the girls were wrong that night, glitter on their cheeks or too jumpy, stupid about movies or already having boyfriends. And then it was late, the ice mostly water in the big glass bowl, like the end of the polar caps. Al kept saying it wasn't time for the cake and then like a song we'd forgotten was even on the mix, you stepped into the house and my whole life.

You looked strong, Ed. I guess you always looked strong, your shoulders and your jaw, your arms leading

15

you through the room, your neck where I know now you like to be kissed. Strong and showered, confident, friendly even, but not eager to please. Enormous like a shout, well rested, able-bodied. Showered I said. Gorgeous, Ed, is what I mean. I gasped like Al did when I gave him the perfect present.

"I love this song," somebody said.

You must always do this at a party, Ed, a slow shrugging path from room to room, nodding at everyone with your eyes on the next place to go. Some people glared, a few guys high-fived you and Trevor and Christian almost blocked them like bodyguards. Trevor was really drunk and you followed him as he slid through a doorway out of view and I made myself wait until the song hit the chorus again before I went looking. I don't know why, Ed. It's not like I hadn't seen you before. Everyone had, you're like, I don't know, some movie everyone sees growing up, everybody's seen you, nobody can remember not seeing you. But just suddenly I really, really needed to see you again right that minute, that night. I squoze by that guy who won the science prize, and looked in the dining room, the den with the framed photos of Al uncomfortable on the steps of church. It was flushed, every room, too hot and too loud, and I ran up the stairs, knocked in case people were in Al's bed already, picked up the cardigan, and then slipped outside for air and in case you were in the yard. And you were, you were. What would bring me to do such a thing, you standing grinning holding two beers with Trevor sick in Al's mom's flower bed? I wasn't supposed to be looking, not for me. It wasn't *my* birthday, is what I thought. There's no reason I should have been out here like this, in the yard, on a limb. You were Ed Slaterton, for God's sake, I said to myself, you weren't even invited. What was wrong with me? What was I doing? But out loud I was talking to you and asking you what was wrong.

"Nothing with me," you said. "Trev's a little sick, though."

"Fuck you," Trevor gurgled from the bushes.

You laughed and I laughed too. You held up the bottles to the porch light to see which was which. "Here, nobody's touched this one."

I don't usually drink beer. Or, really, anything. I took the bottle. "Wasn't this for your friend?"

"He shouldn't mix," you said. "He's already had half a bottle of Parker's."

"Really?"

You looked at me, and then took the bottle back because I couldn't get it open. You did it in a sec and dropped the two caps in my hand like coins, secret treasure, when you handed the beer back to me. "We lost," you explained.

"What does he do when you win?" I asked.

"Drinks half a bottle of Parker's," you said, and then you—

Joan told me later that you got beat up once at a jock party after a losing game so that's why you end up at other

17

people's parties when you lose. She told me it would be hard dating her brother the basketball star. "You'll be a widow," she told me, licking the spoon and turning up Hawk. "A basketball widow, bored out of your mind while he dribbles all over the world."

I thought, and I was stupid, that I didn't care.

—and then you asked me my name. I told you it was Min, short for Minerva, Roman goddess of wisdom, because my dad was getting his master's when I was born, and that, don't even ask, no you couldn't, only my grandmother could call me Minnie because, she told me and I imitated her voice, she loved me the best of anyone.

You said your name was Ed. Like I might not know that. I asked you how you lost.

"Don't," you said. "If I have to tell you how we lost, it will hurt all of my feelings."

I liked that, *all of my feelings*. "Every last one?" I asked. "Really?"

"Well," you said, and took a sip, "I might have one or two left. I might still have a feeling."

I had a feeling too. Of course you told me anyway, Ed, because you're a boy, how you lost the game. Trevor snored on the lawn. The beer tasted bad to me, and I quietly poured it behind my back into the cold ground, and inside people were singing. *Bitter birthday to you, bitter birthday to you, bitter birthday to Al*—and Al never gave me a hard time about

18

staying out there with a boy he had no opinion about instead of coming in to watch him blow out the sixteen black candles on that dark, inedible heart—*bitter birthday to you*. You told the whole story, your lean arms in your jacket crackling and jerky, and you replayed all your moves. Basketball is still incomprehensible to me, some shouty frantic bouncing thing in uniform, and although I didn't listen I hung on every word. Do you know what I liked, Ed? The word *layup*, the sexy plan of it. I savored that word, *layup layup layup*, through your feints and penalties, your free throws and blocked shots and the screwups that made it all go down. The layup, the swooping move of doing it like you planned, while all the guests kept singing in the house, *For he's a bitter good fellow, for he's a bitter good fellow, for he's a bitter good fellow, which nobody can deny*. The song I'd keep, for the movie, so loud through the window your words were all a sporty blur as you finished your game and threw the bottle into an elegant shatter on the fence, and then you started to ask:

"Could I call you—"

I thought you were going to ask if you could call me Minnie. But you just wanted to know if you could call me. Who were you to do that, who was I saying yes? I would have said yes, Ed, would have let you call me the thing I hated to be called except by the one who loves me best of anyone. Instead I said yes, sure, you could call me about maybe a movie next weekend, and Ed, the thing with your heart's desire is that your heart doesn't even know what it desires until it turns up. Like a tie at a tag sale, some perfect thing in a crate of nothing, you were just there, uninvited, and now suddenly the party was over and you were all I wanted, the best gift. I hadn't even been looking, not for you, and now you were my heart's desire kicking Trevor awake and loping off into the sweet late night.

"Was that—*Ed Slaterton*?" Lauren asked, with a bag in her hand.

"When?" I said.

"Before. Don't say *when*. It was. Who invited him? That's *crazy*, him here."

"I know," I said. "Right? Nobody."

"And was he getting your number?"

I closed my hand on the bottle caps so nobody could see them. "Um."

"Ed Slaterton is asking you out? Ed Slaterton *asked* you out?"

"He didn't ask me out," I said, technically. "He just asked me if he could—"

"If he could what?"

The bag rustled in the wind. "If he could ask me out," I admitted.

"Dear God in heaven," Lauren said, and then, quickly, "as my mother would say."

20

"Lauren—"

"Min just got asked out by *Ed Slaterton*," she called into the house.

"What?" Jordan stepped out. Al peered startled and suddenly through the kitchen window, frowning over the sink like I was a raccoon.

"Min just got asked out—"

Jordan looked around the yard for him. "Really?"

"No," I said, "not really. He just asked for my number."

"Sure, that could mean anything," Lauren snorted, tossing wet napkins into the bag. "Maybe he works for the phone company."

"Stop."

"Maybe he's just obsessed with area codes."

"Lauren—"

"He *asked* you *out*. Ed Slaterton."

"He's not going to call," I said. "It was just a party."

"Don't put yourself down," Jordan said. "You have all the qualities Ed Slaterton looks for in his millions of girlfriends, come to think of it. You have two legs."

"And you're a carbon-based life-form," Lauren said.

"Stop," I said. "He's not—he's just a guy."

"Listen to her, *just a guy*." Lauren picked up another piece of trash. "Ed Slaterton asked you out. It's crazy. That's, like, *Eyes on the Roof* crazy."

"It's not as crazy as what is, by the way, a great movie,

21

and it's *Eyes on the Ceiling. And,* he's not really going to call."

"I just can't believe it," Jordan said.

"There's nothing to believe," I said to everybody in the yard, including me. "It was a party and Ed Slaterton was there and it's over and now we're cleaning up."

"Then come help me," Al said finally, and held up the dripping punch bowl. I hurried to the kitchen and looked for a towel.

"Throw those out?"

"What?"

He pointed at the bottle caps in my hand.

"Right, yeah," I said, but with my back turned they went into my pocket. Al handed me everything, the bowl, the towel to dry it, and looked me over.

"Ed Slaterton?"

"Yeah," I said, trying to yawn. I was thumping inside.

"Is he really going to call you?"

"I don't know," I said.

"But you—*hope* so?"

"I don't know."

"You don't know?"

"He's not going to call me. He's Ed Slaterton."

"I know who he is, Min. But you—what are you—?"

"I don't know."

"You know. How can you not know?"

I'm good at changing the subject. "Happy birthday, Al."

Al just shook his head, probably because I was smiling, I guess. I guess I was smiling, the party over and these bottle caps burning in my pocket. Take them back, Ed. Here they are. Take back the smile and the night, take it all back, I wish I could.

This is a ticket for the first movie we saw, see how it says right on it: *Greta in the Wild*, Student Matinee, October 5, a date that'll rattle me forever. I don't know if it's yours or mine, but I know I bought them both and waited outside trying not to pace in the sort-of cold. You were almost late, which turned out to be as usual. I had a feeling. You weren't going to show, was my feeling, the camera sweeping back and forth down the empty street in the movie of the date, *October 5*, me alone, gray, and pacing in the lens. So what, I thought. You're just Ed Slaterton. Show up. Who cares? Show up, show up, where are you? Fuck you, everyone was right about you, prove them wrong, where are you?

And then from nowhere you were in my life again, tapping me on the shoulder with your hair combed and damp, smiling, maybe nervous. Maybe breathless like me.

"Hey," I squeaked.

"Hey," you said. "Sorry I'm late if I'm late. I forgot which theater this was. I never go here. I had it confused with the Internationale."

"The Internationale?" The Internationale, Ed, is not the Carnelian. The Internationale shows British adaptations of the same three novels by Jane Austen over and over again, and documentaries about pollution. "And who was waiting for you at the Internationale?"

"Nobody," you said. "Very lonely. I like it here better."

We stood together and I opened the door. "So you've never been here?"

"Once for a field trip in eighth grade, to see something about World War Two. And my dad took me and Joan before that, before he met Kim it must have been, something in black and white."

"I'm here, like, every week."

"Good to know," you said. "I'll always be able to find you."

"Um," I said, savoring that.

"OK, tell me what we're seeing, again?"

"*Greta in the Wild*. It's P. F. Mailer's masterpiece. Hardly anyone gets to see it on the big screen."

"Uh-huh," you said, looking around the sparse lobby. It was only the usual bearded men struggling in alone, another date couple probably from the university, and an old woman in a beautiful hat that made me stare. "I'll get us tickets."

"I got them already," I said.

"Oh," you said. "Well, what can I get? Popcorn?"

"Definitely. The Carnelian makes the real stuff."

"Great. You like butter?"

"Whatever you want."

"No," you said, and touched me, just on the shoulder, I'm sure you don't remember but it was swoony for me, "whatever *you* want."

What I wanted is what I got. We sat in the sixth row where I always like it. The fading mural, the sticky floor. The bearded men identical and separated in faraway seats, like the corners of a rectangle. The profile of the old woman standing in the back taking off her hat and putting it next to her. And you, Ed, your arm a thrill around me, sitting in the dark as the lights went down.

Greta in the Wild opens, brilliantly, gorgeously, with the curtain opening. Lottie Carson is a chorus girl in a chorus line, with the dimple that made her America's Cinematic Lovely and P. F. Mailer's mistress in all those beautiful parties in the photographs in *When the Lights Go Down: A Short*

Illustrated History of Film, with his arms draped all over her. She's only a little older than I am now, with a lacy fan and a tiny hat and a song called "You're the Pip for Me, Chéri" all flourishy with an orchestra and a glittery cardboard apple that lowers on strings from the rafters. Miles De La Raz can't take his eyes off her, in his skinny waxed mustache and the box seat where he's flanked by scowly bodyguards, and you held my hand with both of your hands, warm and electric with the popcorn abandoned.

Backstage he's an asshole, as if we didn't know from the mustache. "Greta, I told you a million times never to talk to that lousy bum of a trombone player," "Aw Joe, he's just a friend, that's all," etc. More dialogue, another song I think, but—

—you were kissing me. It was sudden, I guess, though it's not sudden to kiss someone on a date, especially if you're Ed Slaterton, and also, if I'm going to write the truth, if you're Min Green. It was a good first one, gentle and jolty, I can feel it now in Al's dad's truck on my neck like light and flutter. What will you do, I asked myself, and then with a *rat-tat-tat* of machine guns laying a curve of bullets into the instrument case in the alley while Lottie Carson screams in her mink, I kissed you back.

Lottie Carson has to leave town, but we stayed right where we were. Miles De La Raz's right-hand man, the bald guy who's also in *Dinner at Midnight* with glasses and a head cold, puts her on the train and she throws her mink in his sputtering face in a pouty huff, but you probably don't remember that scene because by then it was French with your mouth wet and just the slight mint of toothbrushing. Al and I watched it sophomore year, double-featured with *Catch That Gun*, at his house with pizza and iced coffee that made me babbly but Al just trembly nervous with his knee twitching and nowhere to put his hands. So I know the scene. Boy does she regret that gesture with the fur, because the train goes north, way north in a montage I just love, even better on the big screen with the edges of the picture all cloudy, announcing "Buffalo! Next stop Buffalo!" and then the funnier and funnier towns, "Worchester! Badwood! Chokypond! Ducksbreath!" until she's in the goddamn Yukon with Will Ringer all bundled up on a dogsled ready to take her the rest of the way to where she's hiding out, your hand on my neck and me not knowing if you'll slide it down to feel me over my second-favorite top with the weird pearly buttons that mean you have to hand wash it, or just move to hold me at the waist before making your way up underneath, and if I'll stop you, if I want to, if you'll tell anyone, your hands on me and we're only twenty minutes into the first movie of the first date. So I stop the kiss and Lottie Carson sleeps in the igloo alone and Will Ringer, frost on the beard he'll shave off for her, because she asks him to, because he loves her—he sleeps with the dogs. We

29

sat still for the rest, in the dark, merely holding hands until the ending and the big, big kiss, and then we were blinking in the lobby and I asked you what you thought.

"Um," you said, shrugged, looked at me, shrugged again, and shook your hand in a so-so seesaw, and I wanted to grab your wrist and hold your palm right where I'd stopped you from putting it before. My heart, Ed, *thump-thump-thump*ed for it to happen, right then, October 5, at the Carnelian Theater.

"Well, I liked it," I said, hoping I wasn't flushed with thinking it. "Thanks for seeing it with me."

"Yeah," you said, and then, "I mean, you're welcome."

"You're welcome?"

"You know what I mean," you said. "Sorry."

"You meant sorry?"

"*No,*" you said. "I mean, what do we do now?"

"Um," I said, and you looked at me like you didn't know your lines. What could I do with you? I'd been hoping you'd have an idea, the movie was mine. "Are you hungry?"

You smiled gently. "I play basketball," you answered, "so the answer's always yes."

"OK," I said, thinking I could have tea. And watch you eat? Was this the afternoon, the whole October 5? With Greta still dazzling in my brain, I wanted us to do something, I don't know—

And then I gasped, I really did. I had to show you,

because it wasn't something you could see right away, a route to take to a place to go, an opening of the story that could make *October 5* a movie as lovely as the one we'd just seen. It was more than the old woman walking past us, more than anything you could glance at in the normal light of the puddly afternoon. It was a dream of a curtain opening, and I took your hand so I could lead you through it to someplace more than a junior and a senior making out in a theater, somewhere better than tea for the girl and a meal for the athlete like every other afternoon for everyone, something magic on a big screen, something else, something—

—*extraordinary*.

I gasped and pointed the way. I gave you an adventure, Ed, right in front of you but you never saw it until I showed you, and that's why we broke up.

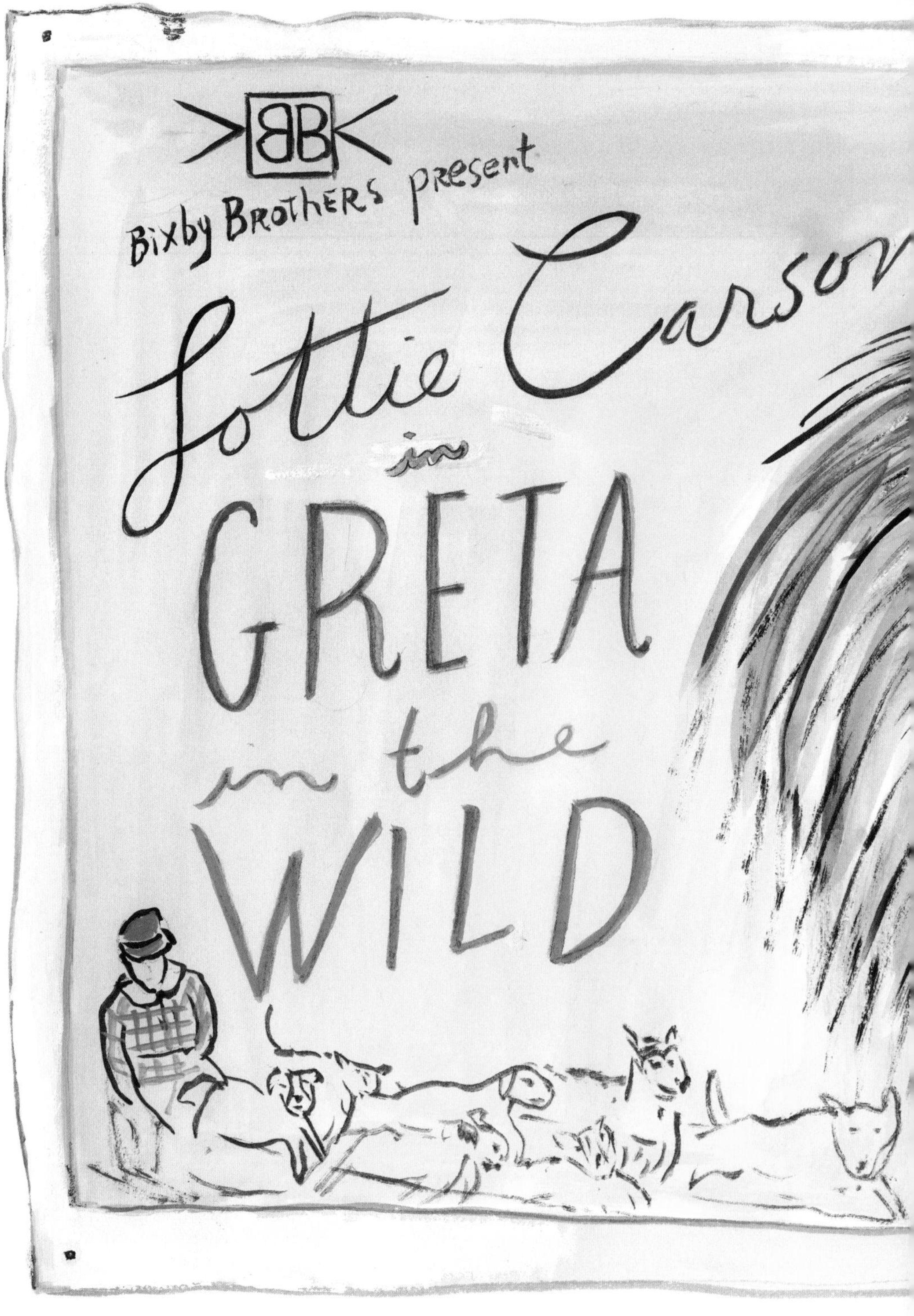
BB
Bixby Brothers present
Lottie Carson
in
GRETA
in the
WILD

It breaks my heart to give this back to you, but you're already heartbroken, so we're even, I guess. Anyway, I can't look at Lottie Carson ever again, for obvious reasons, so if I didn't give this back it would waste away somewhere in a trash heap instead of staring up at you when you open the box and making you cry with her grin, her beautiful grin, the famous grin of Lottie Carson.

"What?" you said, and watched the old woman go down the block.

"Lottie Carson," I said.

"Who's she?"

"From the movie."

"Yeah, I saw her in the back row. With the hat."

"No, that's *Lottie Carson*," I said. "At least I think. Who was *in* the movie. *Greta*."

"Really?"

"Yeah."

"Are you sure?"

"No," I said, "of course I'm not sure. But it could be."

We went outside and you squinted and frowned. "She doesn't look a thing like in the movie."

"That was years and years ago," I said. "You have to use your imagination. If it's her, it means she snuck into the Carnelian to watch herself in the wild, and we're the only people who know."

"If it's her," you repeated. "But how can you be sure?"

"There's no way we can be *sure*," I said. "Not now. But, you know, I had a feeling in there. During the big kiss at the end."

You smiled, and I knew what kiss you were thinking of. "You had a feeling."

"Not *that* kiss," I said, feeling it again, both of your hands holding my hair so dearly out of our faces. "The kiss in the movie."

"Wait a minute," you said, and you went back into the theater. The door swung shut and I watched you through the smudgy glass like a film out of focus, an unrestored print. You stepped quick to the wall and leaned over, and then hurry hurry hurry, you were back out the door and grabbing my arm and we jaywalked across Tenth to the dry cleaner's. I saw the time on the clock on the wall above the rack of clothes that they move around when they're looking for yours. I saw that the movie was short, that I had plenty of time before I told my mom I'd be home and told Al I'd call him with all the details. The clothes moved like they were in a fire drill, filing in an orderly fashion round and round in plastic, and then stopped and an ugly dress reunited with a customer in a crinkly embrace. But you moved my cheek, your hand so warm on me, and I saw what you wanted me to see. Lobby cards, they call them, I know from *When the Lights Go Down: A Short Illustrated History of Film*, you'd snitched the lobby card from the Carnelian. It's a real one, vintage, you can see from the tinting, dimpled and happy in your hand. Lottie Carson with the blizzard in the background, cute as a button in her fur, America's Cinematic Lovely.

"This girl," you said, "this actress and the lady down the street. You're saying they're the same."

"Look at her," I said, and I held the other corner. It took my breath away to touch it. I was holding one corner and you one corner and then one corner had the logo for Bixby Brothers Pictures and one corner is gone, see, ripped and left hanging on a thumbtack in the lobby when you stole it so we could look at Lottie Carson together and see.

"If it's her, then she probably lives here," I realized. She was a little away by now, in the coat, with the hat, halfway to halfway down the block. "Nearby, I mean. Someplace. That would be—"

"If it's her," you said again.

"The eyes look the same," I said. "The chin. Look at the dimple."

You looked down the block and then at me and then at the photo. "Well," you said, "*this* is definitely her. But the lady down the block, that might not be."

I stopped looking at her and looked, my God it was beautiful, at you. I kissed you. I can feel it, my mouth on you, I have a feeling now of the feeling I had then, even though I don't have it anymore. "Even if it isn't," I murmured against your neck when it was through—the dry-cleaning customer *ahem*ed us out of her way with her ugly dress exhausted over her elbow, and I pulled away from you—"we should follow her."

"What? Follow her?"

"Let's," I said. "We can see if it's her. And, well—"

"Better than watching me eat," you said, reading my mind.

"Well, we could have lunch," I said, "instead. Or, if you have to, I don't know. Get home, or something?"

"No," you said.

"No, you don't want to, or no, you don't have to go home?"

"No, I mean yes, OK, if you want to."

You started to cross back to her side of the street, but I took your arm. "No, stay here," I said. "We should follow at a discreet distance." I'd gotten that from *Morocco Midnight*.

"What?"

"It'll be easy," I said. "She walks slow."

"She's old," you agreed.

"She'd have to be," I said. "She'd be something like, I don't know, she was young in *Greta in the Wild* and that was in, let's see." I turned the card over and blinked at a true fact.

"If it's her," you said.

"If it's her," I said, and you took my hand. *And even if it isn't*, I wanted to murmur to your neck again, smelling of your shave and your sweat. Let's go, is what I thought, the movie leaving its vapor trail across my mind. Let's see where this leads us, this adventure with the thrum of the music and the blizzard of stagy snow, Lottie Carson stalking out of the igloo and Will Ringer grumbling and stamping be-fore, of course, he rouses the dogs and *mush!-mush!-mush!*es to find her so Greta will choose the right man, no matter how humble his igloo, her happy tears freezing to diamonds on her dimple in that light only Mailer could get. Let's go, let's go, hurry toward the happy ending with the fur coat of her dreams, pure white polar bear fur Will Ringer tanned himself, wrapped around her so happy and beaming and snug with the engagement ring a surprise in the pocket just as THE END flutters on-screen enormous and triumphant, the big, big kiss. That was the pip for me, chéri. I had a feeling of where it would lead that day, *October 5*, a feeling fanned by the back of this card, the promotional printing of Lottie Carson, a time line with the dates of her life and work. Her birthday was coming up—she was almost eighty-nine. That's what I thought, moving unaware down the street. December 5 is what I saw as we walked together on October 5, let's go, let's go together toward something extraordinary and I started making plans, thinking we would get that far.

If you open this you'll see it's empty, and you'll wonder for a sec if it was empty when you gave it to me—I can see it—another empty gesture you slipped into my hand like a bad bribe. But the truth, and I'm telling you the truth, is that it was full, twenty-four matches lined up cozy inside. It's empty now because they're gone.

I don't smoke, although it looks fantastic in films. But I light matches on those thinking blank nights when I crawl my route out onto the roof of the garage and the sky while my parents sleep innocent and the lonely cars move sparse on the faraway streets, when the pillow won't stay cool and the blankets bother my body no matter how I move or lie still. I just sit with my legs dangling and light matches and watch them flicker away.

This box lasted just three nights, not in a row, before they were all gone and the box held the nothing you see now. The first night was the night of the day you gave it to me, when my mom had finally door-slammed her way to bed and I'd hung up with Al. I was too jitterbuggy happy to sleep, and the whole day kept playing in my brain's little screening room. There's a picture in *When the Lights Go Down: A Short Illustrated History of Film* of Alec Matto smoking in a chair in a room with a slice of light blaring over his head toward a screen we can't see. "Alec Matto reviewing dailies for *Where Has Julia Gone?* (1947) in his private screening room." Joan had to tell me what dailies are, it's when the director takes some time in the evening, while smoking, to see all the footage that was filmed that day, maybe just one scene, a man opening a door over and over, a woman pointing out the window, pointing out the window, pointing out the window. That's dailies, and it took seven or eight matches on the roof over the garage for me to go over our breathless dailies that night, the nervous wait with the tickets in my hand, Lottie Carson heading north on all those trains, kissing you, kissing you, the strange conversation in A-Post Novelties that had me all nerve-wracky after I talked to Al about it, even though he said he had no opinion. The matches were a little *he loves me, he loves me not*, but then

I saw right on the box that I had twenty-four, which would end the game at *not*, so I just let the small handful sparkle and puff for a bit, each one a thrill, a tiny delicious jolt for each part I remembered, until I burned my finger and went back in still thinking of all we did together.

"OK, now what?"

After two blocks Lottie Carson had rounded the corner and stepped into Mayakovsky's Dream, a Russian place with layers and layers of curtains on the window. We couldn't see anything, not from across the street.

"I never noticed this place," I said. "She must be having lunch."

"It's late for lunch."

"Maybe she's a basketball player too, so she eats all the time."

You snorted. "She must play for Western. They're all little old ladies."

"Well, let's follow her."

"In there?"

"What? It's a restaurant."

"It looks fancy."

"We won't order much."

"Min, we don't even know if it's her."

"We can hear if the waiter calls her Lottie."

"Min—"

"Or Madame Carson, or something. I mean, doesn't this

43

look like where a movie star would go, her regular place?"

You smiled at me. "I don't know."

"It totally does."

"I guess."

"It does."

"OK," you said, and stepped into the street, pulling me with you. "It does, it does."

"Wait, we should wait."

"What?"

"It'll look suspicious to go right in. We should wait, like, three minutes."

"Sure, that'll clear us."

"Do you have a watch? Never mind, we'll count to two hundred."

"What?"

"The seconds. One. Two."

"Min, two hundred seconds isn't three minutes."

"Oh yeah."

"Two hundred seconds couldn't be three of anything. It's one-eighty."

"You know, I remember now you are good at math."

"Stop."

"What?"

"Don't tease me about math."

"I'm not teasing you. I'm just *remembering*. You won that prize last year, right?"

"Min."

"What was it?"

"It was just finalist, I didn't win. Twenty-five people got it."

"Well, but the point is—"

"The point is that it's embarrassing, and Trevor and everyone gives me shit about it."

"I don't. Who would do that? It's *math*, Ed. It's not, like, I don't know, you're a really good knitter. Not that knitting—"

"It's as gay as that."

"What? Don't—math's not *gay*."

"It is, kind of."

"Was *Einstein* gay?"

"He had gay hair."

I looked at your hair, then you. You smiled at some gum on the sidewalk. "We really," I said, "live in different, um—"

"Yeah," you said. "You live where three minutes is two hundred seconds."

"Oh yeah. Three. Four."

"Stop it, it's been that already." You led me in a happy jaywalk across, holding both my hands like a folk dance. Two hundred seconds, I thought, 180, what does it matter?

"I hope it's her."

"You know what?" you said. "I do too. But even if it isn't—"

But as soon as we stepped inside, we knew we should step out. It wasn't just the red velvet on the walls. It wasn't just the lampshades, red cloth made rose as the bulbs shone through, or the little glass beads hanging from the shades twirling prismy in the breeze of the open door. It wasn't just the tuxedos of the men whisking around, or the red napkins folded to look like flags with a little twist in the corner for a flagpole, piled on the corner table for replacements, flags on flags on flags on flags like some war was over and the surrender complete. It wasn't just the plates with the red script of *Mayakovsky's Dream* and a centaur holding a trident over his bearded head with one hoof held up to conquer us all and stomp us to meaningless dust. And it wasn't just us. It wasn't just that we were high school, me a junior and you a senior, with our clothes all wrong for restaurants like this, too bright and too rumpled and too zippered and too stained and too slapdash and awkward and stretched and trendy and desperate and casual and unsure and braggy and sweaty and sporty and wrong. It wasn't just that Lottie Carson did not look up from where she was watching, and it wasn't just that she was watching the waiter, and it wasn't just that the waiter was holding a bottle, wrapped in a red folded napkin, tilted high over his head, and it wasn't just that the bottle, iced with a rainy sheen on the neck, was filled with champagne. It wasn't just that. It was the menu, of course of course, presented on a little podium by the door, and how much goddamn everything goddamn cost and how much goddamn money we didn't have on our goddamn selves. So we left, walked right in and left, but not before you grabbed a box of matches from the enormous brandy snifter by the door and pressed it into my hand, another gift, another secret, another time to lean in and kiss me. "I don't know why I'm doing this," you said, and I kissed you back with my hand full of matches on the back of your neck.

The night after I lost my virginity, after you dropped me off and after several blank afternoon hours on my bed tired and restless until I sat up and went outside to watch the sun fall on the horizon—that was another seven or eight matches. And then the third night was after we broke up, which was worth a million matches but instead just took all I had. That night it felt that somehow by flicking them off the roof, the matches would burn down everything, the sparks from the tips of the flames torching the world and all the heartbroken people in it. Up in smoke I wanted everything, up in smoke I wanted you, although in a movie that wouldn't work, even, too many effects, too showy for how tiny and bad I felt. Cut that fire from the film, no matter how much I watch it in dailies. But I want it anyway, Ed, I want what can't possibly happen, and that is why we broke up.

Across the street from Mayakovsky's Dream, right across directly like a Ping-Pong bounce, we hid in A-Post Novelties peeking through the racks of whatnot, waiting and waiting for Lottie Carson to finish her glamorous stopover and leave so we could follow her home. We couldn't loiter on the street, I guess, or who knows why we were in A-Post Novelties with the forever grumpy twin hags who run it, and all the nonsense, expensive and bright, people buy for other people for the other people's birthdays when they don't know each other well enough to know and find and buy what they really want. This camera is at least the only thing you got me from A-Post Novelties, Ed, I'll grant you that. I moved amongst windup animals and dirty greeting cards while you ducked under the mobiles they have until you finally said what it was that was on your mind.

"I don't know any girls like you," you said.

"What?"

"I said I don't know any—"

"Like me how?"

You sighed and then smiled and then shrugged and then smiled. The mobile was silver stars and comets glittering in circles around your head like I'd knocked you silly in a cartoon. "Arty?" you guessed.

I stood right in front of you. "I'm not arty," I said. "Jean Sabinger is arty. Colleen Pale is arty."

"They're freaks," you said. "Wait, are they friends of yours?"

"Because then they're not freaks?"

"Then I'm sorry I said it is all," you said. "Maybe smart is what I mean. Like, the other night you didn't even know we'd lost the game. Usually, I thought everybody knows."

"I didn't even know there was a game."

"And a movie like that." You shook your head and made a weird breath. "If Trev knew I saw that, he'd think, I don't know what he'd think. Those movies are gay, no offense about your friend Al."

"Al's not gay," I said.

50

"The dude made a cake."

"*I* made that."

"You? No offense but it was awful."

"The whole point," I said, "is that it was supposed to be *bitter*, awful like a Bitter Sixteen party, instead of sweet."

"Nobody ate it, no offense."

"Stop saying no offense," I said, "when you say offensive things. It's not a free pass."

You tilted your head at me, Ed, like a dim puppy wondering why the newspaper's on the floor. At the time it was cute. "Are you mad at me?" you asked.

"No, not mad," I said.

"You see, that's another thing. I can't tell. You're a different girl than usual, no offense Min, oops, sorry."

"What are the other girls like," I said, "when they get mad?"

You sighed and handled your hair like it was a baseball cap you wanted to turn around. "Well, they don't kiss me like we were. I mean, they don't anyway, but then they stop when they're mad and won't talk and fold their arms, like a pouty thing, stand with their friends."

"And what do you do?"

"Get them flowers."

"That's expensive."

"Yeah, well, that's another thing. They wouldn't have bought the tickets like you did, for the movie. I pay for everything, or else we have a fight and I get them flowers again."

I liked, I admit, that we didn't pretend there hadn't been other girls. There was always a girl on you in the halls at school, like they came free with a backpack. "Where do you buy them?"

"Willows, over by school, or Garden of Earthly Delights if the Willows stuff isn't fresh."

"Fresh flowers, you're talking about, and you think Al is gay."

You blushed, a dashing red on both cheeks like I'd slapped you around. "This is what I mean," you said. "You're smart, you talk smart."

"You don't like the way I talk?"

"I've just never heard it before," you said. "It's like a new—like for instance a spicy food or something. Like, let's try food from Whatever-stan."

"I see."

"And then you like it," you said. "Usually. When you try it, you don't want the—the other girls."

"What do the other girls talk like?"

"Not a lot," you said. "Usually I guess I'm talking."

"Basketball. Layups."

"Not just, but yeah, or practice, or Coach, if we're gonna win next week."

I looked at you. Ed, you were goddamn beautiful that

day and, you're making me tear up in the truck right now, every other one, too. Weekends and weekdays, when you knew I was looking and when you didn't even guess I was alive. Even with shiny stars bothering your head it was beautiful. "Basketball is boring," I said.

"Wow," you said.

"That's another different thing?"

"I don't like that one," you said. "You never even went to a game, I bet."

"Boys throwing a ball around and bouncing it," I said, "right?"

"And old movies are boring and corny," you said.

"You loved *Greta in the Wild*! I know you did!"

And I know you did.

"I'm playing Friday," you said.

"And I sit in the stands and watch you win and all the cheerleaders scream for you and I wait for you to come out of the locker room standing by myself for a bonfire party full of strangers?"

"I'll take care of you," you said quietly. You reached out and brushed my hair, my ear.

"Because I'd be," I said, "you know, your date."

"If you were with me after the game, it would be more like girlfriend."

"Girlfriend," I said. It was like trying on shoes.

"That's what people would think, and say it."

"They'd think Ed Slaterton was with that arty girl."

"I'm the co-captain," you said, like there was some way someone at school could not know that. "You'd be whatever I told them."

"Which would be what, arty?"

"Smart."

"Just smart?"

You shook your head. "The whole thing of what I've been trying," you said, "is that you're different, and you keep asking about the other girls, but what I mean is that I don't think about them, because of the way you are."

I stepped closer. "Say that one more time."

You grinned. "But I said it so lousy."

What every girl wants to say to every boy. "Say it," I said, "so I know what you're saying."

"Buy something," said the first hag, "or get the hell out of my store."

"We're *browsing*," you said, pretending to look at a lunch box.

"Five minutes, lovebirds."

I remembered to look at the Dream door. "Did we miss her?"

"No," you said. "I've kept an eye out."

"I bet this is another thing you never do."

You laughed. "No, I follow old movie stars most weekends."

"I just want to know where she lives," I said. I felt Lottie Carson's birthday, the back of the lobby card, sparking in my purse, a secret plan.

"It's fine," you said. "It's fun, something. But what will we do when we get there?"

"We'll find out," I said. "Maybe it'll be like *Report from Istanbul*, where Jules Gelsen finds that underground room full of—"

"What is the old movies, with you?"

"What do you mean?"

"What do you mean what do I mean? You talk about old movies with everything. You're thinking about one now probably, I bet."

It was true: the last long shot of *Rosa's Life of Crime*, another Gelsen vehicle. "Well, I want to be a director."

"Really? Wow. Like Brad Heckerton?"

"No, like a *good* one," I said. "Why, what did you think?"

"I didn't really think," you said.

"And what are you going to be?"

You blinked. "Winner of state finals, I hope."

"And then?"

"Then a big party and college wherever they take me, and then I'll find out when I get there."

"Two minutes!"

"OK, OK." You rummaged in a bin of rubber snakes, look busy look busy. "I should get you something."

I frowned. "Everything's ugly."

"We'll find something, it'll kill time. What's good for a director?"

You interviewed me down through the aisles. Masks for actors? No. Pinwheels for background scenes? No. Naughty board games for the party after the awards ceremony? Shut *up*.

"Here's a camera," you said. "There we go."

"It's a pinhole camera."

"I don't know what that is."

"It's cardboard." I didn't tell you that I didn't know what it is either, just read it on the side of the thing. Or, until now, the truth of it, that I knew of course, of course I knew it, that there was a game and that you'd lost that night I met you in Al's yard. But you seemed to like, I think, I hoped back then, that I was different.

"Cardboard, so what, I bet you don't even have a camera."

"Directors don't do the cameras. That's for the DP."

"Oh right, the DP, I almost forgot."

"You don't know what a DP is."

Three of your fingers gave me a jumpy tickle, right in the belly, where the butterflies lived. "Don't start with me. Alley-oops, technical fouls, I have a dictionary of basketball in my head, and you don't know any of it. I'm buying you this camera."

"I bet you can't even take real pictures with that."

"It comes with film, it says."

"It's cardboard. The pictures wouldn't come out right."

"It'll be, what's the French word? For weirdo movies?"

"What?"

"There's a, you know, an official descriptive phrase."

"Classic films."

"No, no, not gay ones like your friend. Like, really, really weird ones."

"Al is not gay."

"OK, but what is it? It's French."

"He had a girlfriend last year."

"OK, OK."

"She lives in LA. He met her at a summer thing he did."

"OK, I believe you. Girl in LA."

"And I don't know what French thing you mean."

"It's for super-weird films, like oh no, she's falling up the staircase inside somebody's eye."

"How would you know, anyway, if there was some film thing?"

"My sister," you said. "She was almost a film major. She goes to State. You should talk to her, actually. You remind me, a little bit—"

"This is like hanging out with your sister?"

"Wow, this is another time when I can't tell if you're mad."

"Better buy me flowers just in case."

"OK, you're not mad."

"Out!" shrieked the second twin like a bossy curse.

"Ring this up," you said, and tossed her the camera for her to catch. And here it is back at you, Ed. I could see the little arrogance there, from co-captaining, how it really could be *whatever you told them*, like you said. Girlfriend, maybe. "Ring this up and leave us alone."

"I don't have to put up with this," she snarled. "Nine fifty."

You gave her a bill from your pocket. "Don't be that way. You know I love you best."

That was the first time I saw that part, too. The hag melted into a fluttery puddle and smiled for the first time since the Paleozoic era. You winked, took the change. I should have seen it, Ed, as a sign that you were unreliable. Instead I saw it as a sign of charming, which is why I didn't break it off right then and there, like I should have and wish wish wish I did. Instead I stayed out late with you on a bus and the stranger streets of a lost, far neighborhood where Lottie Carson was hiding out in a house with a garden full of statues making shadows in the dark. Instead I just kissed your cheek for a thank-you note, and we walked out opening the package and reading the instructions together for how to do it. It's easy, it was easy, too easy to do this. *Avant-garde* was the term you were thinking of, I learned from *When the Lights Go Down: A Short Illustrated History of Film*, but we didn't know that when we had this. There were a million things, every-thing, I didn't know. I was stupid, the official descriptive phrase for happy. I took this thing I'm giving you back, this thing you gave me as the star we were waiting for finally emerged.

"It's opening!"

"Where?"

"No, the door!"

"What?"

"Across the street! It's her! She's leaving!"

"OK, let me open it."

"Hurry!"

"Be quiet about it, Min."

"But this is the moment."

"OK, let me read the directions."

"No time. She's putting on gloves. Act normal. Take the

picture. It's the only way we can know if it's her."

"OK, OK, *Wind film tight with knob A.*"

"Ed, she's going."

"Wait." Laughing. "Tell her to wait."

"What, wait, we think you're a movie star and want to take your picture to be sure? I'll do it, give it to me."

"Min."

"It's mine anyway, you bought it for me."

"Yeah, but—"

"You don't think girls can work a camera?"

"I think you're holding it upside down."

Ten steps down the block, laughing more.

"OK, *now*. She's going around the corner."

"Hold subject in frame—"

"Open the thing."

"How?"

"Give it back."

"Oh, like this. *Now. There.* Then what? Wait. OK, yes."

"Yes?"

"I think so. Something clicked."

"Listen to you, *something clicked*. Is this how you'll be when you're directing a movie?"

"I'll order someone else to do it. Some washed-up basketball player."

"Stop."

"OK, OK, then you wind it again? Right?"

"Um—"

"Come on, you're good at *maaath*."

"Stop it, and this isn't math."

"I'm taking another. There, at the bus stop."

"Not so loud."

"And another. OK, your turn."

"My turn?"

"Your turn, Ed. Take it. Take some."

"OK, OK. How many are there?"

"Take as many as we can. Then we'll get them developed and then we'll see."

But we never did, did we? Here it is undeveloped, a roll of film with all its mysteries locked up. I never took it anyplace, just left it waiting in a drawer dreaming of stars. That was our time, to see if Lottie Carson was who we thought she was, all those shots we took, cracking up, kissing with our mouths open, laughing, but we never finished it. We thought we had time, running after her, jumping on the bus and trying to glimpse her dimple through the tired nurses arguing in scrubs and the moms on the phone with the groceries in the laps of the kids in the strollers. We hid behind mailboxes and lampposts half a block away as she kept moving through her neighborhood, where I'd never been, the sky getting dark on only the first date, thinking all the while we'd develop it later. We searched her mailbox, *Lottie Carson* on the envelope we hoped, you sprinting to trespass on her worn and ornate porch, perfect for her, while I waited with my hands on the fence watching you bound your way there and back. You clambered there in five swift secs, over the iron wrought spikes cooling my palms in the dusk, quick quick quick through the garden with the whatnot of gnomes and milkmaids and toadstools and Virgin Marys all outwitted like the opposing team. You flew your way through all those stone silent statues, and if I could I'd thunk them all at your goddamn doorstep, as noisy as you were quiet, as furious as we were giggly, as cold and scornful as I was breathless and hot watching you cat burglar for evidence and come back shrugging and empty-handed so we still didn't know, we still couldn't be sure, not until everything was developed. Those thick kisses on the long bus home at night with nobody but us leaned out on the last row of seats and the driver with his eyes on the road knowing it was none of his business, and kissing more at the bus stop when we parted from that date, and the shout of you moving crisscross away from me after I wouldn't let you walk me home and have my mom bullet you all over the sidewalk from asking where in the world I had been. "See you Monday!" you called out, like you'd just figured out the days of the week. We thought we had time. I waved but couldn't answer, because I was finally letting myself grin as wide as I'd wanted all afternoon, all evening, every sec of every minute with you, Ed. Shit, I guess I already loved you then. Doomed like a wineglass knowing it'll get dropped someday, shoes that'll be scuffed in no time, the new shirt you'll soon enough muck up filthy. Al probably heard it in my voice when I called him, waking him because it was so late, then telling him never mind, forget it, sorry I woke you, go to bed, no I'm fine, I'm tired too, try you tomorrow, when he said he had no opinion. Already. First date, what could I do with my stupid self and the thrill of *see you Monday*? thinking there was time, plenty of time to see what pictures we'd made? But we never developed them. Undeveloped, the whole thing, tossed into a box before we really had a chance to know what we had, and that's why we broke up.

Here it is. It took me forever to get it back to how it was, your amazing math scores all adding up in how this thing was folded. When I opened my locker Monday morning, it looked like an origami spaceship from the old Ty Limm sci-fis had landed on top of *Understanding Our Earth*, ready to unleash the electro-decimator onto Janet Bakerfield's spinal column and destroy her brain. That's what this did to me, too, when I unfolded the note and read it. I got all tingly and it made me stupid.

Maybe you waited for me that first morning at school, I never asked you. Maybe you wrote it last minute after second bell and slipped it through the slats before the Olympic dash to homeroom all the jocks always do, leaving the slowpokes spinning as you bound past their backpacks like pinball toys. You didn't know I never go to my locker until after first. You never really learned my schedule, Ed. It is a mystery, Ed, how you never knew how to find me but always found me anyway, because our paths tug-of-warred away from each other for the whole loud and tedious stretch of school, the mornings with me hanging out with Al and usually Jordan and Lauren on the right-side benches while you shot warm-up hoops on the back courts with your backpack waiting with the others and skateboards and sweatshirts in a bored heap, not a single class in common, your Early Lunch trash-dunking your apple core like it's part of the same game, my Late Lunch on the weird corner of the lawn, hemmed in by the preppies and the hippies bickering over the airwaves with competing sound tracks except on hot days, when they truce it with reggae. In *Ships in the Night*, Philip Murray and Wanda Saxton meet in the last scene under the rainy awning, their wrong wife and fiancé finally story-lined away, and walk out together into the downpour—we know from the first scene, Christmas Eve, that both of them like walking in the rain but don't have anybody who will do it with them—and it's the miracle of the ending. But there are no crisscross intersections for us, a blessing now that I live in fear of bumping into you. We'd only meet on purpose, after school before practice, you changing quick and shooing away your warm-upping teammates until you had to go, one more kiss, had to, one more, OK now really, I really really have to go.

And this note was a jittery bomb, ticking beneath my normal life, in my pocket all day fiercely reread, in my purse all week until I was afraid it would get crushed or snooped, in my drawer between two dull books to escape my mother and then in the box and now thunked back to you. A note, who writes a note like that? Who were you to write one to me? It boomed inside me the whole time, an explosion over and over, the joy of what you wrote to me jumpy shrapnel in my bloodstream. I can't have it near me anymore, I'm grenading it back to you, as soon as I unfold it and read it and cry one more time. Because me too, and fuck you. Even now.

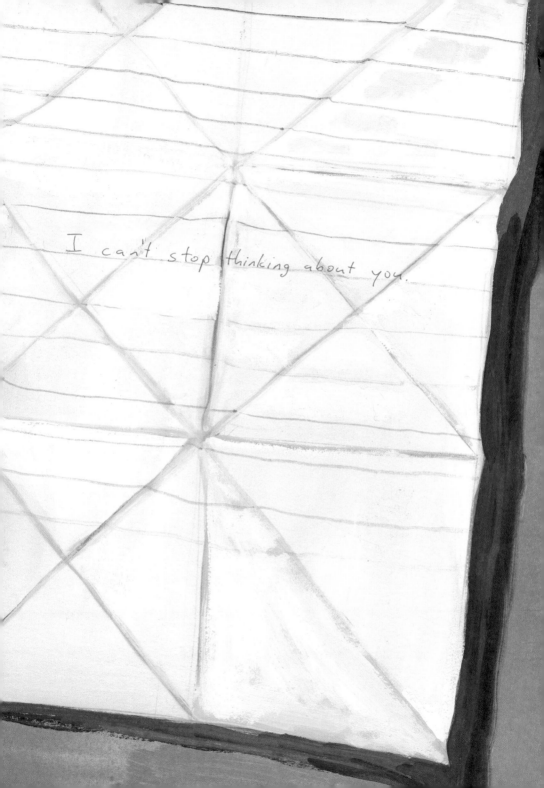

I can't stop thinking about you.

When I look at this ripped in half, I think of the travesty of what you did and the travesty of how I didn't care at the time. I can't look at this while I write about it, because I'm afraid Al will see and we'll have to talk about it all over again, like you've ripped it in half all over again and all over again I said nothing. You probably think this is from the night we went to the Ball, but it isn't. You probably think it got ripped in half by accident, for no reason, just the way things happen with all the posters for all the events that end up pulped by rain or untaped by the janitors to make room for the next one, like the Holiday Formal posters that are everywhere up now, with Jean Sabinger's careful drawing of one of those glass ornaments which, if you look real close, has people dancing all funhouse-curved in a reflection, replacing the skulls and bats and jack-o'-lanterns on this poster, but you did it, bastard. You did it and made a scene.

Al had the posters in a huge orange stack on his lap on the right-hand benches when I arrived at school with my hair ridiculous damp and my Advanced Bio homework not done in my backpack. Jordan and Lauren were there, too, each holding—it took me a sec to get it—a roll of tape.

"Oh no," I said.

"Morning, Min," Al said.

"Oh no. Oh no. Al, I forgot."

"Told you," Jordan said to him.

"I totally forgot, and I need to find Nancie Blumineck and *beg* to copy her bio. I can't! I can't do it. Plus, I don't have any tape."

Al took out a roll of tape, he'd known all along. "Min, you swore."

"I know."

"You swore it to me three weeks ago over a coffee *I bought you* at Federico's, and Jordan and Lauren were witnesses."

"True," Jordan said. "We are. We were."

"I notarized a statement," Lauren said solemnly.

"But I *can't*, Al."

"You swore," Al said, "on Theodora Sire's gesture when she throws her cigarette into what's-his-name's bathwater."

"Tom Burbank. Al—"

"You swore to help me. When I was informed that it was mandatory that I join the planning committee for the All-City All Hallows' Ball, you didn't have to swear to attend all the meetings like Jordan did."

"So *boring*," Jordan said, "my eyes are still rolled into the back of my head. These are glass replicas, Min, placed in the gaping bored holes in my skull."

"Nor did you have to swear, as Lauren did, to hold Jean Sabinger's hand through six drafts of the poster as each of the decorations subcommittee submitted their comments, two of which made her cry, because Jean and I still can't talk after the Freshman Dance Incident."

"It's true, the crying," Lauren said. "I have personally wiped her nose."

"Not true," I said.

"Well, it's true she cried. And Jean Sabinger is a *crier*. It's these artistic temperaments, Min."

"All you swore to do," Al said, "in order to get your free tickets by being a listed member of my subcommittee, was to spend one morning taping up posters. *This* morning, actually."

"Al—"

"And don't tell me it's stupid," Al said. "I am Hellman

High junior treasurer. I work in my dad's store on weekends. My entire life is stupid. The All-City All Hallows' Ball is stupid. Being on the planning committee for *anything* is the height of stupidity, even when, especially when, it's mandatory. But stupidity is no excuse. Although I myself have no opinion—"

"Uh-oh," Jordan said.

"—some would argue, for instance, that a certain amount of stupidity is exhibited by anyone who finds it necessary to chase after Ed Slaterton, and yet I abused my power just yesterday, as a member of the student council, and looked up his phone number in the attendance office at your request, Min."

Lauren pretended to faint dead away. "*Al!*" she said, in her mother's voice. "That is a violation of the student council honor code! It will be a very long time before I trust you ever, ever—OK, I trust you again."

They all looked at me now. Ed, you never cared for a sec about any of them. "OK, OK, I'll tape up posters."

"I knew you would," Al said, handing me his tape. "I never doubted you for a second. Pair up, people. Two will do gym through library, the others the rest."

"I'm with Jordan," Lauren said, taking half the stack. "I know better than to interfere with the sexual tension festival you and Min have going on this morning."

"*Every* morning," Jordan said.

"You think everything's sexual tension," I said to Lauren, "just because you were raised by Mr. and Mrs. Super-Christian. We Jews know that underlying tensions are always due to low blood sugar."

"Yeah, well, you killed my Savior," Lauren said, and Jordan saluted good-bye. "Don't let it happen again."

Al and I headed for the east doors, stepping over the legs of Marty Weiss and that Japanese-looking girl who holds hands with him by the dead planters, and we spent the morning excused from homeroom taping these posters up like they meant something, Al holding them flat and me zipping out pieces of tape over the corners. Al told me some long story about Suzanne Gane (driver's ed, bra clasp) and then said, "So, you and Ed Slaterton. We haven't talked much about it, really. What's—what's—?"

"I don't know," I said, *tape tape.* "He's—it's going well, I think."

"OK, none of my business."

"Not that, Al. It's just, it's, you know, he's—fragile."

"Ed Slaterton is fragile."

"No, *we* are. I mean. Him and me, it feels that way."

"OK," Al said.

"I don't know what will happen."

"So you won't become one of those sports girlfriends in the bleachers? *Good shot, Ed!*"

"You don't like him."

"I have no opinion."

"Anyway," I said, "they don't call it *shot.*"

"Uh-oh, you're learning basketball terminology."

"Layups," I said, "is what they say."

"The caffeine withdrawal is going to be hard," Al said. "No after-school coffee served in the bleachers."

"I'm not giving up Federico's," I said.

"Sure, sure."

"I'll see you there *today.*"

"Forget it."

"You don't like him."

"No opinion, I said. Anyway, tell me later."

"But Al—"

"Min, behind you."

"What?"

And there you were.

"Oh!" It was too loud, I remember.

"Hey," you said, and gave a little nod to Al that of course embarrassed him with his Halloween stack.

"Hey," I said.

"You're never around here," you said.

"I'm on the subcommittee," but you just blinked at that.

"OK, will I see you after?"

"After?"

"After school, are you going to watch me practice?"

After a sec I laughed, Ed, and tried the ambidextrous

thing of looking at Al with a *Can you believe this guy?* and you with a *Let's talk later* at the same time. "*No,*" I said. "I'm not going to *watch you practice.*"

"Well, then call me later," you said, and your eyes flitted around the stairwell. "Let me give you the best number," you said, and without a thought, Ed, the travesty occurred, and you ripped down a strip from the poster we'd just put up. You didn't think it, Ed, of course you didn't, for Ed Slaterton the whole world, everything taped up on the wall, was just a surface for you to write on, so you took a marker from behind Al's ear before he could even sputter, and gave me this number I'm giving back, this number I already had, this number that's still a poster in my head that'll never tear down, before giving back the pen and ruffling my hair and bounding down the stairs, leaving this half in my hand and the other wounded on the wall. Watching you go, Al watching you go, watching Al watching you go, and realizing I had to say you were a jerk to do that and not being able to make those words work. Because right then, Ed, the day of my last coffee after school with Al at Federico's before, yes, goddamnit, I started to sit in the bleachers and watch you practice, the number in my hand was my ticket out of the taped-up mornings of my life, my usual friends, a poster announcing what everybody knows will happen because it happens every year. *Call me later,* you'd said, so I could call you later, at night, and it is those nights I miss you, Ed, the most, on the phone, you beautiful bastard.

Because the day, it was school. It was the bells too loud or rattly in broken speakers that would never get fixed. It was the bad floors squeaky and footprinted, and the bang of lockers. It was writing my name in the upper right-hand corner of the paper or Mr. Nelson would automatically deduct five points, and in the upper left-hand corner of the paper or Mr. Peters would deduct three. It was the pen just giving up midway and scratching invisible ink scars on the paper or suiciding to leak on my hand, and trying to remember if I'd touched my face recently and am I a ball-point coal miner on my cheeks and chin. It was boys in a fight by the garbage cans for whatever reason, not my friends, not my crowd, my old locker partner crying about it on the bench I sat on freshman year with a gang I barely see anymore. Quizzes, pop quizzes, switching identities during attendance when there's a sub, anything to pass time, more bells. It was the principal on the intercom, two whole minutes of ambient hum and shuffling, and then a very clear "That's on, Dave" and it clicking off. It was a table selling croissants for French Club knocked over by Billy Keager like always, and the strawberry jam a sticky stain on the ground for three days before anyone cleaned it. Old trophies in a box, a plaque with this year's names waiting to be filled in on the tag, blank and coffin-shaped. It was the deep daydream and waking up with a teacher wanting an answer and refusing to repeat the question. Another bell, the announcement "ignore that bell" and Nelson scowling "He said *ignore* it" to people zipping backpacks. It was the paperwork in homeroom, stapled together wrong so everyone has to rotate them to fill them out. It was the bullshit and the tryouts for the school play, the banners with the big game Friday and then the big banner stolen and the announcement to rat someone out if anyone knew anything. It was Jenn and Tim breaking up, Skyler getting his car taken away, the rumor that Angela was pregnant but then the counter-rumor, no, it's the flu, everyone throws up with the flu. It was the days the sun wasn't even trying to get out of the clouds and be nice for once in its starry life. It was wet grass, damp hems, the wrong socks I forgot to throw out and so now found myself wearing, the sneaky leaf falling from my hair where it had nested for hours to surely someone's delight. Serena getting her period and not having anything for it like always, scrounging from girls she didn't even know in the bathrooms during second. Big game Friday, go Beavers, beat them Beavers, the dirty joke so boring to everyone but freshmen and Kyle Hapley. Choir tryouts, three girls selling knitting to help people in a hurricane, it was the library having nothing to offer no matter what needed looking up. It was fifth period, sixth, seventh, clock-watching and cheating on tests just because why not. It was suddenly being hungry, tired, hot, furious, so unbelievably startling sad. Fourth period, how could it be only fourth, is what it was. Hester Prynne, Agamemnon, John Quincy Adams, distance times rate equals something, lowest common whatever, the radius, the metaphor, the free market. Someone's red sweater, someone's open folder, it was wondering how someone could lose a shoe, just one shoe, and not see it when it was hopeful on the windowsill for weeks. Call this number on the bulletin board, call if you've been abused, if you want to kill yourself, if you want to go to Austria this summer with these other losers in the picture. It was *STRIVE!* in bad letters on a faded background, *WET PAINT* on a dry floor, big game Friday, we need your spirit, give us your spirit. Locker combinations, vending machines, hooking up, cutting class, the secrets of smoking and headphones and rum in a soda bottle with mints to cover the breath, that one sickly boy with thick glasses and an electronic wheelchair, thank God I'm not him, or the neck brace, or the rash or the orthodontics or that drunk dad who showed up at a dance to hit her across the face, or that poor creature who somebody needs to tell *You smell, fix it, or it will never, never, never will it get better for you.* The days were all day every day, get a grade, take a note, put something on, put somebody down, cut open a frog and see if it's like this picture of a frog cut open. But at night, the nights were you, finally on the phone with you, Ed, my happy thing, the best part.

82

The first time I called your number it was like the first time anyone had called anyone, Alexander Graham Whatsit, married to Jessica Curtain in the very dull movie, frowning over his staticky attempts for months of montage before finally managing to utter his magic sentence across the wire. Do you know what it was, Ed?

"Hello?" Damn it, it was your sister. How could this be the best number?

"Um, hi."

"Hi."

"Could I speak to Ed?"

"May I ask who's calling?"

Oh, why did she have to do that, is what I thought, picking at my bedspread. "A friend," I said, stupid shy.

"A friend?"

I closed my eyes. "Yes."

There was an empty, buzzy moment and I heard Joan, though I didn't know Joan yet, exhale and debate whether to question me further, while I thought, I could hang up now, like a thief in the night in *Like a Thief in the Night*.

"Hold on," she said, and then a few secs, hum and clatter, your voice distant saying "What?" and Joan's mocking, "Ed, do you have any friends? Because this girl said—"

"Shut up," you said, very close, and then "Hello?"

"Hey."

"Hey. Um, who—"

83

"Sorry, it's Min."

"Min, hey, I didn't recognize your voice."

"Yeah."

"Hold on, I'm moving to another room because *Joanie's just standing here!*"

"OK."

Your sister saying something something, running water. "They're *my* dishes," you said to her. Something something. "She's a *friend* of mine." Something something. "I don't know." Something. "Nothing."

I kept waiting. *Mr. Watson,* is the first thing the inventor said, miraculously from another room. *Come here—I want to see you.* "Hey, sorry."

"It's OK."

"My sister."

"Yeah."

"She's—well, you'll meet her."

"OK."

"So—"

"Um, how was practice?"

"Fine. Glenn was kind of a dick, but that's usual."

"Oh."

"How was—what is it that you do, after school?"

"Coffee."

"Oh."

"With Al. You know, hanging out. Lauren was there too."

"OK, how was it?"

Ed, it was wonderful. To stutter through it with you or even stop stuttering and say nothing, was so lucky and soft, better talk than mile-a-minute with anyone. After a few minutes we'd stop rattling, we'd adjust, we'd settle in, and the conversation would speed into the night. Sometimes it was just laughing at the comparing of favorites, I love that flavor, that color's cool, that album sucks, I've never seen that show, she's awesome, he's an idiot, you must be kidding, no way mine's better, safe and hilarious like tickling. Sometimes it was stories we told, taking turns and encouraging, it's not boring, it's OK, I heard you, I hear you, you don't have to say it, you can say it again, I've never told this to anyone, I won't tell anyone else. You told me that time with your grandfather in the lobby. I told you that time with my mother and the red light. You told me that time with your sister and the locked door, and I told you that time with my old friend and the wrong ride. That time after the party, that time before the dance. That time at camp, on vacation, in the yard, down the street, inside that room I'll never see again, that time with Dad, that time on the bus, that other time with Dad, that weird time at the place I already told you in the other story about that other time, the times linking up like snowflakes into a blizzard we made ourselves in a favorite winter. Ed, it was everything, those nights on the phone, everything we said until late became later and then later and very late and finally to go to bed with my ear warm and worn and red from holding the phone close close close so as not to miss a word of what it was, because who cared how tired I was in the humdrum slave drive of our days without each other. I'd ruin any day, all my days, for those long nights with you, and I did. But that's why right there it was doomed. We couldn't only have the magic nights buzzing through the wires. We had to have the days, too, the bright impatient days spoiling everything with their unavoidable schedules, their mandatory times that don't overlap, their loyal friends who don't get along, the unforgiven travesties torn from the wall no matter what promises are uttered past midnight, and that's why we broke up.

LET'S STAY IN THAT
PLACE ALONE

This is what I'm talking about, Ed: the truth of it. Look at this coin. Where is it from? What prime minister, whose king is that? Somewhere in the world they take this as money, but it wasn't that day after school at Cheese Parlor.

We'd agreed, with more debate and diplomacy than that Nigel Krath's seven-hour miniseries on Cardinal Richelieu, that we'd have an early dinner or a post-coffee, post-practice snack or whatever you call it when it's sunset and you're really supposed to be home but instead you're having waffle-iron grilled cheeses and scalding watery tomato soup at a place of neutral territory. They were tired of not meeting you, even though it hadn't been any time at all. They thought, all of them, Jordan and Lauren, except Al because he had no opinion, that I was hiding you. Or was I ashamed of my friends? Was that it, Min? I said you had practice and they said that was no excuse and I said of course it was and then Lauren said maybe if we didn't invite you, like with Al's party, maybe then you'd show up, so I said OK, OK, OK, OK, shut up, OK, Tuesday after your practice, after coffee at Federico's, let's go to Cheese Parlor, which is centrally located and equally despised by everyone, and then I asked you and you said sure, sounds good. I sat in a booth with them and waited. The booths crinkled and the place mats suggested we quiz each other with cheese facts.

"Hey, Min, true or false, parmesan was invented in 1987?"

I took my finger out of my gnawing mouth and gave Jordan a strong flick. "You're going to be nice to him, right?"

"We're always nice."

"No, you never are," I said, "and I love you for it, sometimes, mostly, but not today."

"If he's going to be your whatever he's going to be," Lauren said, "then he should see us as God supposedly made us, in our natural environment, with our usual—"

"We never come here," Al said.

"We already argued this out," I reminded him.

Lauren sighed. "All I mean is that if we're all going to hang together—"

"Hang together?"

"Maybe we won't," Jordan said. "Maybe it won't be that way. Maybe we'll just see each other at the wedding, or—"

"Stop it."

"Doesn't he have a sister?" Lauren said. "Think of both of us dressed together for the bridal party! In *plum*!"

"I knew it would be like this. I should tell him not to come."

"Maybe he's already scared of us and won't show," Jordan said.

"Yeah," Lauren said, "like maybe he didn't want Min's number and maybe he wasn't going to call her and maybe they're not really—"

I put my head down on the table and blinked at a picture of brie.

"Don't look now," Al murmured, "but there's a ball of sweat by the entrance."

It's true you looked particularly, wetly athletic. I stood up and kissed you, feeling like the scene in *The Big Vault* where Tom D'Allesandro doesn't know Dodie Kitt is being held hostage right under his nose. "Hey," you said, and then looked down at my friends. "And hey."

"Hey," they all goddamn said.

You slid in. "I haven't been here in forever," you said.

"Last year I went with somebody who liked the whatsit, the hot cheese soup."

"Fondue," Jordan said.

"Was that Karen?" Lauren said. "With the braids and the cast on her ankle?"

You were blinking. "That was Carol," you said, "and it wasn't the fondue. It was the hot cheese soup." You pointed to HOT CHEESE SOUP on the menu and it got, just for a sec, quiet as death.

"We always get the special," Al said.

"I'll have the special, then," you said. "And Al, don't let me forget." You tapped your bag. "Jon Hansen told me to give you a folder for the lit project."

Lauren swiveled to Al. "You have lit with Jonathan Hansen?"

Al shook his head and you took a long, long gulp of ice water. I watched your throat and wanted it, every word you ever said, all to myself. "His girlfriend," you explained finally. "Joanna Something-ton. Though, and don't tell anyone, not for long. Hey, you know what I remember?"

"That Joanna Farmington's a friend of mine?" Lauren said.

You shook your head and waved to the waiter. "Jukebox," you said. "They have a good jukebox here." You heaved your bag onto the table, found your wallet, frowned at the bills. "Somebody have change?" you said, and then reached across for Lauren's purse. I don't know a thing about sports, but I could feel the strike ones, strike twos, strike threes whizzing over your head. You undid the zipper and moved things around. My eyes met Al trying not to meet my eyes. The person besides Lauren who is allowed into Lauren's purse is whoever finds her dead in a ditch and is looking for identification. A tampon peeked out the top and then you found her change purse and smiled and unsnapped it and dumped the coins into your hand. "We all want the special," you told the waiter, and then you stood up and strode to the jukebox, leaving me alone at a shell-shocked table.

Lauren was staring at her purse like it was dead in the road. "Jesus Christ and his biological Father."

"As your mother would say," Jordan added.

"They do that," I said desperately, "with their friends, share money like that."

"*They do that?*" Lauren said. "What is this, a nature special? Are they hyenas?"

"Let's hope they don't mate for life," Jordan muttered.

Al just looked at me, like he'd jump on his horse, fire his revolver, open the escape hatch, but only on my say-so. I didn't say-so. You came back and grinned at everybody and, strike billion, Tommy Fox started to play. Ed, I can't even explain, but Tommy Fox, I never told you, is a joke to us, not even a good joke because Tommy Fox is too easy a joke.

You grinned again and spun this coin on the table, sputter spin sputter spin, while we all stared.

"This didn't work," you said, pointing to the middle of the table, the no-man's-land where this useless thing was spinning.

"You don't say," Lauren said.

"I love the guitars on this," you said, sitting down and throwing your arm around me. I leaned against it, Ed, your arm felt good even with Tommy Fox in the air.

"He's joking," I said. Desperately again. I hoped and lied, Ed, for you. This clattered to a stop and I pocketed it while we ate and stuttered and stumbled and paid and left. Your eyes were so sweet, walking me to the bus while they walked the other way. I watched them huddled together and already laughing. Oh, wherever it works, Ed, I thought with your hand on my hip and the not-fitting coin in my pocket. Wherever it's good, whatever strange faraway land, let's go there, let's stay in that place alone.

Look close and you'll see the hair or two that came with the rubber band when you ripped it off me. Who would do such a thing? What kind of man, Ed? I actually didn't mind at the time.

Our first time where you live, where you'll read this, heartbroken. Walking home with you for the first time, the bus together, after watching you practice. I was worn out, tired from not having my usual Federico's coffee. Tired from being bored, really, in the bleachers while you practiced free throws with the coach blowing his shrieky whistle with the advice of *Try to get it in the basket more*. I actually dozed for a sec on your arm on the bus, and when I woke up you were looking wistful at me. You were sweaty and a mess. I felt my breath bad from sleeping even for that minute, the way it does. The sun came through the smeared and messed-up transit windows. You said you liked watching me sleep. You said you wished you could see me wake up in the morning. For the first time, not for the first time if I'm going to tell the real truth, I tried to think of someplace, someplace extraordinary, where that would happen. The whole school knows that if we make state finals, everyone from the team stays in a hotel and Coach looks the other way, but we never made it that far.

When we walked through the back door, you called out "Joanie, I'm home!" and I heard someone, "You know the rules—don't talk to me until you shower."

"Hang out with my sister for a sec?" you asked me.

"I don't know her," I said, in a living room with all the sofa cushions pushed together on the floor like dominoes.

"She's nice," you said. "I told you about her. Talk about movies you like. Don't call her Joanie."

"But *you* called her Joanie," I said, but you were off bounding up the stairs. The sofa gutted of cushions, stacks of distant magazines, a teacup, the whole room unsupervised. Through the doorway was music I instantly loved but couldn't really pin down. It sounded like jazz but not embarrassing.

I walked toward the tune, and Joan was dancing in the kitchen with her eyes closed, partnered with a wooden spoon. Chopped piles were everywhere on the counter. Ed, your sister is beautiful amazing, tell her that from me.

"What is this?"

"What?" She wasn't surprised or anything.

"Sorry. I like the music."

"You shouldn't be sorry to like this music. Hawk Davies, *The Feeling*."

"What?"

"*You either have the feeling or you don't.* You haven't heard of Hawk Davies?"

"Oh yeah, Hawk Davies."

"Stop it. It's cool you haven't. Ah, to be young again."

She turned it up and kept dancing. I could, I thought, maybe should go back into the living room. "You're the girl from the phone the other night."

"Yeah," I owned up.

"A *friend*," she recited. "What's your name, *a friend*?"

I told her it was Min, short for etc.

"That's quite a speech," she said. "I'm Joan. I like Joanie like you like Minnie."

"Ed told me, yeah."

"Don't trust the word of a boy who's sweaty filthy at the end of *every goddamn day take a goddamn shower!*"

She shouted the last of this at the ceiling. *Stomp stomp*

stomp, rattle of the kitchen light fixture, and upstairs the shower went on. Joan grinned and then looked me over on the way to go back to chopping. "You know, I hope you don't mind, and no offense, but you don't look like a sidelines girl."

"No?"

"You're more—" *chop chop* she searched for the *chop chop* word. Behind her was a rack of knives. If she said *arty*—

"—interesting."

I made myself not smile. *Thank you* didn't seem right for it. "Well, today I was a sidelines girl," I said. "I guess."

"Hey!" She perked up bright and sarcastic, her eyes wide and the knife up like a flagpole. *"Let's watch boys practice playing a game so we can watch them play the game later!"*

"You don't like basketball?"

"Sorry, did you like it? How was it, watching him?"

"Boring," I said instantly. Drum solo on the album.

"Dating my brother," she said, with a shake of her head. She stepped to the stove and stirred and licked the spoon, something tomato. "You'll be a widow, a basketball widow, bored out of your mind while he dribbles all over the world. So you don't like basketball—"

It was already true, Ed. I had already wondered if it was OK to do homework or just read while you practiced. But nobody else was. The other girlfriends didn't talk much among themselves and never to me, just looking my way like the waiter had brought the wrong salad dressing. But it was so elegant and worthwhile to have you wave, and the sweat on your back when you all divided into shirts and skins.

"—and don't know music, what do you like?"

"Movies," I said. "Film. I want to be a director."

Song stopped, next one began. Joan looked at me for some reason like I'd socked her. "I heard," I said. "Ed told me you were studying film. At State?"

She sighed, put her hands on her hips. "For a little bit. But I had to change. Get more practical."

"Why?"

The shower turned off. "Mom got sick," she said, flicking her chin in the direction of the far bedroom, and there's something that never came up with you, not on any night on the phone.

But I'm good at changing the subject. "What are you making?"

"Vegetarian Swedish meatballs."

"I cook too, with Al."

"Al?"

"My friend. Can I help you?"

"All my *life*, Min, for *eons* I have waited for someone to ask that question. I hope you agree that aprons are useless, but here, take this." She went to the door and fiddled at the knob for a sec before dropping it into my hand. Rubber bands, you kept them there, every doorknob in the house.

"Um."

"Put your hair up, Min. The secret ingredient is not *your hair*."

"Then how do you make vegetarian Swedish meatballs? Fish?"

"Fish is meat, Min. Oyster mushrooms, cashews, scallions, paprika I need to find, parsley, grated root vegetables, which you can grate. The sauce I did already, that's bubbling. Sound good?"

"Yes, but it's not really very Swedish."

Joan smiled. "It's not really very *anything*," she admitted. "I'm just trying something here, you know? *Attempting* is what I'm doing."

"Attempted meatballs, you could call it instead," I said, with my hair up.

She handed me the grater. "I like you," she said. "Tell me if you want to borrow my old Film Studies books. And tell me if Ed treats you badly so I can fillet him," so I guess you're on a plate somewhere with lemon and whatnot, Ed. Instead you came downstairs with crazy hair and loose clothes, a T-shirt from a stadium show, bare feet, and shorts.

"Hi," you said, and wrapped your arms around me. You gave me a kiss and took the rubber band, *ow*, out of my hair.

"*Ed.*"

"I like it better, no offense, it looks better down."

"She needs it up," Joan said.

"No, we're hanging out," you said.

"Yes, and cooking."

"You could at least put on decent music."

"Hawk Davies crushes Truthster like a grape. Go watch TV. Min's helping me."

You pouted to the fridge and grabbed milk to drink from the carton and then pour in a bowl for cereal. "You're not my real mom," you said, obviously an old joke.

Your beautiful sister took the rubber band out of your hand and dropped it into mine, a loose worm, lazy snake, wide-open lasso ready to rodeo something. "If I were your real mom," she said.

"Yeah, yeah, strangled in the crib." You snacked off to the living room, and Joan and I made the vegetarian Swedish meatballs, which turned out delicious and surprising. I told Al the recipe that night, and he said they sounded great and maybe we could make them Friday night or Saturday or Saturday night or even Sunday night, he could ask his dad for the night off from the shop, but I said no, I wasn't going to be free all weekend, it was a busy weekend for me. My calendar was full, not that I have a calendar. You slumped stretched out on the cushions, what they were doing on the floor, with cereal and dumb TV I could see but not hear from the kitchen. Cooking with Joan like she was my sister too, kind of, simmering and warm and scented like pepper and sweetness and smoke, dancing finally next to her. Hawk Davies giving me the feeling, giving everybody the feeling that afternoon in your kitchen. Letting my hair down with my hair up, in a rubber band from your doorknob, and your shirt riding up as you hung out on the floor, your shorts loose and low, the small of your back I'd watched all day.

Take it back, Ed. Take it all back.

I guess I was supposed to put this up, I guess it should have hung over my bed in a crisscross diagonal like it was X-ing out anything else: HELLMAN HIGH SCHOOL BEAVERS. And I guess I could say the reason it never went anywhere was that the Beaver colors of yellow and green clashed with what is over my bed, the poster of my favorite movie in the world, *Never by Candlelight*, Theodora Sire's eyebrows forever raised in the poster Al gave me last birthday that took him forever to find, like she wasn't going to say anything but that what went on in my bedroom was inelegant and unworthy of me. I didn't put it up, didn't want it up, should have known then.

It might as well have said HELLMAN HIGH SCHOOL ED'S NEW GIRLFRIEND when I found it Friday staked in a slat in my locker, waving in the breeze of the stale vents like when the diplomats arrive in *Hotel Continental*. It took some wiggling to get it out, and I felt my flushy face grinning and fighting not to grin. Everybody knows that even though the pennants are always for sale on game days with the second-string cheerleaders assigned to hawk them desperate and smiley in the cafeteria, they're only for freshmen and parents and any other clueless souls and for the girlfriends of the players who snitch them to give out like long-stemmed roses Friday morning. And people saw and worked it out. Jillian Beach had nothing flying at her locker, and enough people had gossiply seen me with you at practice that week after school to figure who my flag was from. The co-captain, must have been somewhere in the gasping, and Min Green. People must have asked Lauren, asked Al if it was true. They must have said *yeah*, just *yeah*, or maybe they said worse, I don't like to think.

And inside my locker, the ticket. You probably didn't pay for that either. I don't know how it works, with the reserved section roped off for friends and family, guarded by the boys from the JV team all fluffed out with the importance of their security jobs. Those tickets are long gone now, torn and burned into nothing and smoke. You told me later that you were sorry there wasn't an extra for Al but of course he could come to the party after or wherever we went if we lost, but anyway Al told me he had plans, no, thanks. When I got to my seat, Joan was my date, with some biscotti in tinfoil, still warm.

"Ah, a pennant," I remember she said. "Now everybody knows what side you're on, Min."

She had to yell to talk to me. A dad behind us put his hand on my shoulders, *Be seated, be seated, even though the game hasn't started I need a perfect unobstructed view of a shiny wood floor with girls and pom-poms jiggling away.*

"Go Beavers, I guess," I said.

"It's the 'I guess' that makes it such a great cheer."

"Well, it's—" I wanted to say *my boyfriend's*, but I was afraid Joan would correct me. "Ed's thing. I'm trying to be nice. And he gave me it."

"Of course he did," Joan said, and folded open the tinfoil. "Have some biscotti. I tried walnuts instead of hazel, tell me what you think."

I held them in my hands. Joan hadn't been home the rest of our first week, leaving me alone reading in your discombobulated living room while you showered. Although you'd invited me upstairs. But I was afraid she'd come home, I didn't know what the rules were, so I waited until you came downstairs still damp from the shower and we lay together on the cushions on the floor with the TV talking over us. I can tell you the truth, which is that I liked it better when you helped me touch you, running our hands over and inside your clean clothes, than when you touched me, so unsure I was about when Joan might come home and see us.

"Are you going to the party after?"

"Me?" Joan said. "No, I'm done with bonfires, Min. I go to some of the games, about half, don't want to be a bad sister, but the parties afterward are his responsibility, I tell him. I tell him, no coming home so late he sleeps through Saturday; no not coming home; if he throws it up, he cleans it up."

"Sounds fair."

"Tell him that," Joan said with a snort. "He wants no rules and breakfast in bed."

You bounded out as they said your name through a thing blaring professional with enthusiasm. My ears ached from how loud they loved you, the ball you caught from the coach throwing it sideways, *dribble dribble* as if the whole place wasn't roaring, and then a layup and it looked iffy from where I sat but it went in and the roof blew off the place and you clowned and bowed and beat on Trevor grinning and then, like Gloria Tablet must have felt when she served coffee to Maxwell Meyers and found herself screen-testing the next day, then you pointed at me, right at me, and grinned and I froze and waved my flag until the next thing was announced and you threw the ball *hard* at Christian with an impy smile.

"See what I mean?" Joan said.

"Maybe I can whip him into shape."

She put her arm around me. She was wearing something, I could smell the scent of it, or maybe it was just the cinnamon or nutmeg of cooking. "Oh, Min, I hope so."

The rest of the team was announced. Blowing whistles. I thought for a sec, for some reason, that I'd cry at what Joan had said, and I flapped my pennant to evaporate my teary eyes. "But if you do," she warned, "or if you don't, don't keep him too long past midnight."

"You're not my real mom," I was brave enough to say, and then stupid enough and realized it was the wrong joke. Yours, your joke with Joan, but she frowned and looked out at the pom-poms. There was a silence, except for everyone screaming.

"These are good," I said about the cookies, code for *sorry*.

"Yeah, well," she said, and patted my hand for *I forgive you*, but that was definitely the wrong joke, "don't eat them all," and the game started. The roar and the boom was like nothing I'd known, even when I was a freshman and went to the first pep rally because I had the wrong first friends and didn't know any better. The whole gym was *alive* with it, cheering and waving and gripping their friends, bells when someone scored, drowned out by screams, delighted or disappointed depending whose side you were on. Whistles and then sweaty slowdowns, glares, shrugs, long-armed gestures of *aw, shucks* when it was a penalty or an error. Everyone's hands palm out on the court, the ball is mine, the basket, the point, the score, the team, the game, losing you in the skinny pack, finding you again, letting go of you to check the numbers up on the wall. It was a rush, Ed, and I loved the rush, stomping my feet on the bleachers to help with the thunder, until my eyes found the clock and it was only a meager fifteen goddamn minutes that had gone by. I'd thought maybe we were almost done, the air hissing out of me and the pennant suddenly a barbell too heavy to lift again. Fifteen minutes, just, how could it be only that? I blinked at the time to make sure, and Joan was grinning, catching me. "I know, right?" she said. "These take forever. It's like the dictionary definition of hurry up and wait." I'd lost track of you long enough that when I found you again my brain said, *Why are you watching this guy? Who is he? Why this guy and not other guys, any other one?* because there was something wrong with the picture I was in. It was like an apple running for Congress, a bike rack wearing a bathing suit. I was cut and pasted wrong into a background you could immediately — or, anyway, after fifteen minutes — see didn't match up, was how I felt. Like Deanie Francis in *Midnight Is Near* or Anthony Burn as Stonewall Jackson in *Not on My Watch*, wrong for the part, ill cast. My backpack, I wondered — with homework and the Robert Colson book I'd loaned Al that he'd finally given back added to the weight heavy against my legs—would I have to take it with me for the loud night looming obvious ahead of us since the score had tipped overwhelmingly ahead? What to do with this pennant and its plastic stick to hold it, do you throw them in the fire, why did nobody ever have a pennant at a party? What was I, wrong, doing here in the gym, never a voluntary place for me? They didn't even sell coffee and I wanted one, boy, did I want one then, ready to bash the exhausted mom and snatch her thermos of it. But there was no way to escape, out the windows too high and not even open, crumbs and walnuts at my feet, Christian's brother leaning against me accidentally, Joan laughing with someone's mom on the other side. You don't leave; you stay. I thought I was keeping quiet, but gradually my throat was hoarse and hot from all my yelling. I spaced out and came to, caught you pointing at me again and hoped I hadn't missed other times, you smiling up to find me only to see me scowling, bored, and eyes elsewhere. I tried, I tried again, waving my flag like a hostage. I gave you my spirit and you won.

The score was a billion to six, and no surprise. Everyone on earth would never starve and forever find love and happiness, since we won, but if we'd lost, they would have gouged out our eyes and thrown us naked onto hot coals and poisonous snakes for all the cheering and hugging at the end, strangers hugging like the end of *The Omega Virus* when Steve Sturmine finds the antidote. The biggest ones

113

for you, Ed, realizing as you victory-lapped that I should have bought flowers and hidden them someplace to shower them down upon you, now that the Beavers had won and, according to everybody but the boredom-stricken arty girl in the reserved seats who was fat from too many biscotti, saved the entire human race. I'm sorry—then I was sorry, but not now—but it was boring to me. "Not too late!" Joan reminded me as we crowded out, waving to her car as I waited for you to come out excited and clean, my brave boy with a new girlfriend, happy with your teammates. But it *was* too late. I had to stay and I stayed, knowing, understanding, liking none of it. Not until the other girlfriends slipped the pennant off the stick did I know to toss mine into the trash with the others. Then I rolled up my flag while they rolled up theirs, agreeing it was a good game, a fun time, a perfectly acceptable thing to do with my Friday night. I waited for you, Ed, to make it all worthwhile, and when you kissed me and said "I told you you'd like it," that was the only part I liked. But I just kissed you, too, and let you hoist my back-pack with yours onto your beautiful shoulders and walked next to you, my fingers sweaty on the scroll of the pennant, not knowing where to put my hands as we grouped up in the parking lot to carpool to Cerrity Park. What else could I do? There was no choice, as far as I could think. You won the game, we won the game, the party afterward, the drinking, the big blaze, and finally alone someplace too late, I had no choice, not from the moment I first saw this flag fly. I had no choice. We weren't going to sneak off to the movies instead, just talk anywhere, someplace else. Not the co-captain, not that night, not with me the new girlfriend, and that's why we broke up.

This is like the truck I'm in, never thought of that until now. I'm rattling along in this truck, writing to you with this tiny truck in my other hand, Al next to me keeping quiet and letting me finish breaking up with you, holding this toy and wondering if I can say everything about it, the entire truth. It makes me feel like an experimental animated film I saw as part of Annualmation Fest at the Carnelian, a girl in a truck holding a truck, inside the truck another girl holding another truck, etc. Dumping you times infinity. Still not enough.

Who knows where things come from, really? When we

got to the park that night, the fire was already going, the hooting and hollering. We'd been in the back of somebody's little car, scrunched and kissing even though there was one more person, Todd, I think, but not the Todd I know, in the backseat next to us. When the car stopped, it was something wondrous ahead of us in the windshield, the bright orange and the flicker-flicker of shadows dashing in front of it like a documentary about the lousy day coming up when the sun explodes and the human race calls it quits. But it was just the fire, and people running in front of it, drunk already or just wild and frantic and free. My face must have shown that I thought it was beautiful and gorgeous.

"I told you," you said. "I knew you would like this."

You kissed me and I let you think, wanted to agree, that you were right. "It'd be a great opening shot," I admitted, staring out. "Wish I had a camera."

"I bought you a camera," you said.

"Slaterton spent money?" if-it-was-Todd said. "Like, his own money from his own wallet? This must be serious."

"It *is* serious," I said, and reached across you, opened the door, why not, let that rock ripple the pond this weekend. Stars were out, even, and the air cold from one angle where the night kept watch and the wall of heat from the fire coming the other way at us. You stretched your way out of the car and there was a roar, all hail the conquering co-captain, from the party. Two girls had a stuffed greyhound, a hulking gray toy like a spoiling uncle would give, and threw it into the bonfire to spark and sizzle: the enemy mascot. The eyes gleamed plastic and unflammable, *Get me out of here*. But there was only another cheer and horns from arriving cars, and then of course the music sprang up, lousy rock as bold and dull as a giant potato. "Love this song," Todd said, like it was unusually brave to like what was number one on the radio, and he started singing along, *There's a storm raging inside my heart, tell me you and I will never part*, etc. The grunts who always bring the beer played invisible drums. Awful but perfect, I had to admit, I can see the movie with the exact same thing going. You held me then let go.

"Do *not* put this down," you said, slipping my backpack onto my shoulder. "Don't put anything down you don't want in the fire. I'm getting us beer."

"You know I don't like it," I said. By now I'd told you about dumping the Scarpia's at Al's Bitter Sixteen.

"Min," you said, "you *really* don't want to be sober for this," and you jaunted off, having a point, I thought. I stood for a sec wondering *now what?* and thought about sitting on some logs felled nearby, like some pioneers had canceled a cabin last minute, but *don't put anything down you don't want in the fire*, I remembered, and, anyway, the great flames were beckoning with their sheer light, inescapable and mighty. I stepped closer, closer still, the camera I could see close on my face, letting the shivering light of the fire make a nice visual on my brow. Searched my pockets for something I could add. Found my ticket, the one you left for the game, made it smoke in a sec. Kept staring, still staring, the fire so glorious in my eyes that the music started sounding good, even. Stared some more, my brain so deep in the bonfire that I startled hard at the hand on my shoulder.

"Almost too close," said Jillian Beach, your goddamn ex-girlfriend. "Your first bonfire, right?"

"Sort of," I said, feeling my arms cross.

"We knew it," said the girl who was with her. "It always happens, getting too close when someone's never seen it before. It's like the fire attracts the virgins, ha-ha."

They were both looking slyly at me. I wanted a beer. "Ha-ha," I said. "It's true my hymen is extremely flammable."

They laughed, but only sort of. "Okaaay," Jillian said, with that weird curve she uses in her voice sometimes, airy but spiky like a bug-eating plant. "That was kinda funny but kinda weird."

"Happens all the time," I said, another movie I love that you'll never see.

They looked me over. Both of them were skinnier, and at least one of them, not Jillian, was also prettier. "I'm Annette," that one said.

"Min," I said, yanking back my hand when I saw we weren't supposed to shake. "Short for Minerva, Roman goddess of—"

"Okaaay," Jillian said in that way again. "First, everyone knows you, they all found out. And B, when you meet somebody, you don't have to give a whole speech, history of the world. Min is fine. Later people can hear your medical history."

"Jillian's drunk," Annette said quickly. "Also, you know, she and Ed used to go out."

"Like *last week*," Jillian said. "You say it like it was the eighteen-whatevers."

"This is her first bonfire, since," Annette said. "You know, it's hard for her."

"You're making it hard," she spat.

"Jillian—"

"I didn't even want to go over to her. I *didn't*."

"I'll get her out of here," Annette said to me.

"I don't need your help getting out of here," she said, though her tipsy stomp called that a lie. "Nice to meet you, Greek goddess of bye-bye."

She waggled her fingers, and her beer frothed over the thick rings on her hands, the kind of jewelry all wrong for me. Annette stepped closer and we watched her go through a plume of sudden smoke—the wind changed, I guess.

"Sorry."

"No, it's fine," I said. "I love being in a soap opera."

"Kinda no choice tonight," Annette said. "When Jillian does her vodka thing . . ."

"I know I'm stupid about my name," I said to my shoes. "I learned it a long time ago and I just keep saying it. I should stop."

"No, it's cool."

"No, I sound like an idiot."

"Well, it's cool your name has a story. I'm just Annette, like a little Ann, you know? If you can't afford the regular Ann, there's Ann-*ette*, marked down."

"There's Annette DuBois," I said.

"Oh yeah, who's she again?"

"An old movie star," I said. "Did you ever see *Call Me a Cab*? Or *Night Watchgirl*?"

Annette shook her head. Somebody tossed planks into the fire, but you could still smell the pot from behind a bush.

"*Call Me a Cab*'s so great. Annette DuBois plays the dispatcher, flirting with everybody through the car radios. She likes Guy Oncose best, but one day this actress gets into his cab and makes him read from the script so she can practice her home-wrecker scene, and Annette DuBois hears them and thinks he's a cad."

"Like a driver?"

"No, *cad*, it means an asshole. A guy who's mean to women."

"That's everybody." She took a long sip.

"Well, Annette starts giving him the bad jobs, like driving to the wrong part of town, and she's living with her mom who's played by Rose Mondrian who's always great."

"OK, OK, I'll see it."

"She's so beautiful. You could, she has this hat she wears, Annette DuBois, I mean, you'd look great in."

She smiled at me, her teeth so shiny they showed little parts of the bonfire. "Really?"

"Absolutely," I said, and where was my boyfriend?

"Ed's right about you," she said. "You're different."

"Arty," I said. "I know. Can I have some of yours?"

She handed me the plastic cup. "He never said arty."

"What did he say?"

"Just different. He likes you, Min."

I sipped, I liked beer, hated beer, sipped again. "I didn't realize you were close."

"I'm, like, the only ex-girlfriend he talks to."

"Oh," I said. I'd forgotten, if I ever knew, but then re-membered what everybody knew and stood biting my lips next to her, grateful that the bonfire made everyone, not just me, appear to be blushing.

"Oh," she said back at me.

"Sorry, I—"

"It's OK."

"Annette, I didn't think."

"Right. You remember something else besides an old movie now, huh?"

"I'm sorry."

"You already said that, and I already said OK. Junior prom was a long time ago."

"Yeah."

"Yeah," she said. "So we keep in touch, me and Ed."

"That's good."

"That's what everybody says. The least we could do, or something, or me. Like it means it didn't happen, or happened less, anyway. Anyway, we're nice to each other, and he says really nice things about you."

"Well, thanks."

"Thought you should know," Annette said. Her eyes were shiny in the night as we were quiet together watching the fire, and I finished her beer instead of saying something more. I kept thinking, I thought of everything. I thought of *Three Lost Brides*, in which the women who've all been married to the same man meet accidentally and then shriek at each other and then plan his murder and then—unsatisfying in the movie, with Al snorting derisive about it—forgive him and hold hands in the credits. The ex-girlfriend club, I thought, Ed Slaterton Chapter; I'd have to join eventually if I had to think about it, not like we were going to be forever. I mean, who would dare think that, *forever*? Some idiot girl who wouldn't know how things played out. I thought how I only wave at Joe if I see him in the halls, how that can't even count as still talking to him, let alone staying friends like we promised we would when we ended it. But most of all, in the blaze and clatter of the park, I tried to put it together how I saw it then and how I saw it before, turning it over like a toy in my hand, the way it's different again now with you, with your friends gone from my Fridays and no more bonfires lighting up my eyes in the park and you just an ex-boyfriend about to get his stuff thrown back on his doorstep. Because right then, the planks collapsing and the sparks jumping up to the moon, you were my date for the night, and your friends, your exes, were like old wooden stairs, unreliable and full of strange creaks, only certain ones I could trust and only after testing them to find out. It was a world I was in, shouty with mascots and nowhere to put my stuff if I didn't want it burned away. But before, not so long ago—my own rose from prom still OK on the mirror, dried but not a corpse—you were just Ed Slaterton, jocky hero, handsome in the student newspaper and star of a million strands of gossip. Now Annette was a person to me, standing right there, and not just an *oh-my-God-have-you-heard*, and you were something else fierce and fiery in my chest and I tried to put it together in my head, the print and the negative, the boyfriend and the celebrity shadow, like Theodora Sire sat next to me in history, borrowing pencils, but was still a movie star above my bed. Because as you came out of the dark to me, you were the boy I was kissing and wanted to kiss more, back to find me at a party like anybody might do, but you were Ed Slaterton too, and not the cad you are now, but just Ed Slaterton, co-captain, with a beer in your hand and Jillian Beach on your arm.

"OK," she was saying. "See? She's fine. You can talk to me for a minute without your precious *Minerva* disappearing."

"Jesus Christ, Jillian," Annette said.

"Hi," you said to me. "Sorry that took a while. I got you a beer."

"Got one already," I said, holding up my empty cup.

"Then that one's mine," Jillian said, grabbing your hand holding it. You moved away but, Ed, not fast enough, so it was Annette who came to the rescue.

"Come on," she said, already dragging Jillian. "We'll both get beers."

"They only give the captain the good stuff," she said.

"Co-captain," you said, idiot, very wrong answer.

"*Jillian*," Annette said. "See you later, Min."

"*Min*," Jillian sneered. "The artsy fag hag at a bonfire. How long can this thing go?" but Annette got her out of there like snarling Doris Quinner at the end of *Truth on Trial*. I tossed my empty cup. You gave me the beer you'd brought.

"I'm really sorry," you said.

"It's OK" is what came out of my teeth.

"I know you're mad at me," you said. "I should have kept you next to me. Everyone wanted to say hello. They do it every game I win."

"OK."

"But I wanted to find you this surprise, is where I went."

"Surprise!" I said. "A beer at a bonfire!"

"Not that."

"Surprise!" I said. "Your ex-girlfriend yelling drunk at me!"

You shook your head. "She's," you said, "well, she's OK, Jillian, but you can't seriously be jealous. Look at her."

"Most people would say," I said, "that she's beautiful."

"That's because she's been with most people," you said.

"Including *you*."

You shrugged at me, like you couldn't help it, she was right there on the plate. But then you took your other hand from behind your back and rolled this into my hand, small, heavy, cold, your fingernails dirty, your fingers curled around it until I held it up to the light of the fire.

"Toy truck," I said, but the truth I'm telling you is that I'm lousy at the pout, already warming to you knowing this would smooth it fine.

"I know it's stupid, kinda," you said, "but I always look for them here. And you, Min, you are the only girl, *person*, who would even get this. I mean, no offense. Wait, forget I said that last thing, shit. But you are, Min."

I could not, of course not, *not* smile at you. "Tell me," I said.

You sigh-shrugged. "Well, kids lose them. Boys. They

bring them, their favorites anyway, to play traffic-jam pileup over by the wall there, the curved part by where the sand is, you know? See?"

You were pointing at sheer blackness, nothing at all in that direction in the dark. *See?* You'd said "traffic-jam pile-up" like it was a real thing everyone said, "World War Two" or "love at first sight."

"And—?"

"*And*, it's like I used to," you said. "I'd do it, and of course sometimes lose them, or a kid snitches them, bigger, like a bully, or you just forget them buried in a pile of sand. But, Min, I know it's lame, but those were my saddest times. I'd cry my eyes out when I realized, beg my mom in the middle of the night to take me back here to find them. Nobody got it, *it's just a toy* or *you have plenty of cars* or *it's your responsibility to take care of your things*. But I was so lost without them, those times when I lost them. So now I always look and I *always*, Min, you can *always* find at least one. And I know it's weird, or mean, even, because I should probably leave them there in case, although they were always gone, of course, if I ever got to go back in the morning. I'd give them back if I could, I wouldn't torture someone like that, whatever boy lost them. But this feels better, like the right thing. I find them and I look, I've always looked, for someone to give them to, who didn't think Slaterton was crazy. I know it's stupid, like some-how I can make it right, all the ones I lost, it's stupid—"

128

I was kissing you by now, one hand tight around the little truck and the other in your hair, still short and still no combing like the little boy you were, crying in this same park. Hard I kissed you, like that too, would make it right, the right thing to do this wild, strange Friday night.

"How do you like your first bonfire?" you said in my ear.

"It got better," I said.

More kissing, more.

"But tomorrow we'll do my end of it?" I said. "Tomorrow?"

"Your end?"

Trying not to think of Jillian (*How long can this thing go?*), my friends frowning with their bad grilled cheese. "My turn, my side, however you want to say it. Like, of the see-saw. The thing *I* want to do."

"Another movie?"

"If there's time, but Tip Top Goods for sure, remember? I told you, and you said Joan would let you have the car."

"Yes. Whatever you want."

"Tomorrow."

"Tomorrow."

More.

"But tonight's not over," you said.

"Yes. What do we —"

"Well, Steve has his car."

"Are we leaving already?"

You looked, Ed—*right at me.* "No," you said, and I nodded, not trusting my mouth to say anything, just take another sip. Though of course it did more. We got to Steve's car. This is another thing I think of, turning it over, try to put together two pictures of it, but this time it's about me, it's myself I'm trying to figure. Because one sounds so disgusting, not even able to tell Al about it, win the big game, take the virgin to her first bonfire, feed her a beer or two, and then the two of us in someone's car with your hand between my legs, unbuttoned and hiked down and the noises I made, before I finally, gasping, stopped you. It sounds terrible and it's probably the truth, the real picture, gross when I write it down and shamed about it. But it's the real, whole truth I'm trying to get down, how it happened, and honestly it felt different then, different from that bad picture. I can see it, so gentle the way you moved, the thrill that was there with us as no one knew where we were or what we were doing. It was different, Ed, and beautiful how we moved and touched, not just two kids fooling around like it would look in a movie. Even now that is the one I try to see, not just the kissing and the clothing and the quiet, taut, and awkward afterward, wondering how late it was, thanking the gods for no cruel laughing knock on the window. Not just that, but the things I can't see, can't bear to, and the things I didn't see until I finally got home and turned on the bathroom light, first to look at my reflection and then at my strange hand hurting with odd, skinny bruises on my palm, sore, almost breaking the skin. I can feel them now almost, as I hold this, the marks left from the way my hand clenched so tight and ragged with breath and wild joy in the back of that car, around this odd, thrilling thing you gave me that I can't stand to look at ever again.

Ed, did you ever see—no, of course you didn't—*Like Night and Day*, this Portuguese vampire movie the Carnelian ran for a full week? Of course you didn't see it. I saw it twice. A girl—I don't know the actors, they're all Portuguese—has a dull job as a clerk in some government thing and walks home through a graveyard dreaming. One day, she works late, and it's night. The nighttime scenes are in black and white. She meets the boy vampire, slender and pale with his eyes glassy and angry, and for a while she's with him every night and spends her days squinting and exhausted and pale and almost getting fired. Her blind mother senses something wrong, *spiritual unrest* is what the subtitle says she says. This music plays, and the girl dreams what he also dreams, crying in his grave, a gauzy dance of Catholicism and spinning skulls that I don't really get. Then *she's* a vampire, and he's a young man with amnesia in a hospital who finally gets discharged and finds work as a clerk, and the affair begins again until one day, announced at the government office as dreamed by the blind mother, there's an eclipse and it ends in tragedy and ashes. When I dragged Al along so I could see it a second time, he finally said, when I told him there was no way someone could see *Like Night and Day* and not have an opinion, he said his opinion was that it should have been called *We Fuck at Dusk*. And it's true the love scenes are in a strange light, an in-between space as the characters bump and adjust to their haze of a dream of a life. It was like that then, the same lighting when you picked me up at seven at Steam Rising, my third-favorite coffee place but the best one near my house. The Portuguese lovers part dazed and bitten, not knowing what would happen next, I didn't know either, what the encounter would be in the weird dawn. The streets were graveyard quiet and we'd fooled around in Steve's car and maybe I'd messed it all up, I thought, missed my cues, unaware at the bonfire the way you slapped my friends with a jukebox choice. Or maybe I was just tired. I was hoping it would work, that it was still working, but maybe it had changed since you'd dropped me off at one in the morning. Just tired, I thought, waiting worried under the awning, the raging rain not helping a bit, and then hurried to your sister's car when you pulled up, the umbrella tucked under my arm because I couldn't hold it up and both our coffees too.

"Hey," you said, "I mean, good morning."

"Hey," I said. I made a motion with my wet face, like *let's just pretend we kissed.*

"I can't believe it."

"What?"

"*What?* How early it is. What did you think?"

"Well, this is the thing with Tip Top Goods. It's magical, but the hours are like, undead. Saturdays only, seven thirty to nine AM."

"So you've been there before?"

"Just once."

"With Al."

"Yeah, why?"

"Nothing. It's just—"

"What?"

"You gave me a hard time last night, with Jillian."

"Yelling at me all drunk, yeah."

"But you talk about Al all the time and I'm not supposed to get jealous, I'm just saying."

"Jealous? I never went out with Al. He's a friend, just friends. It's different."

"OK, not jealous, but not even feel weird about it, I guess is what I mean."

"Because he's *not*, he wasn't a boyfriend."

"If he's not gay and he hung out with you the whole time, he wanted to be. It's boyfriend or want to be boyfriend or I guess gay. Those are the choices."

"What? Where did you learn that?"

You gave me a cranky smile. I stopped gripping the coffees so hard, let the umbrella clatter into my lap. "Hellman High School," you said.

"Well, those aren't the choices," I said. "There's friends."

"OK."

"OK, so—"

"What?"

"What—why—"

"Why am I acting like this?"

I braced myself, almost closed my eyes. "Yeah."

You gave me a sighing smile. "Tired, I guess. It's early."

"OK, that's why I brought you coffee."

"I don't drink coffee."

I had to stare at you a sec. *"What?"*

You shrugged and spun the wheel. "Never got into it."

"*Into* it? Have you ever *had* coffee?"

"Yes."

"Really?"

You stopped at the yellow light, peered out at the world

between swipes of the wipers. I took a sip of mine. It was early for me too. I'd just had time to shower and scrawl a *going out* to my mom, luckily I'd thought to choose my clothes when we finally said good night and I paced around my room thinking about us. "No," you said finally. "I mean, not really. Yes, sips, of course I've had it. But I always, I mean I never liked it, so when everyone's having it, I—" You sighed with your teeth showing.

"What?"

"I throw it out."

I smiled at you.

"What?"

"Nothing," I said.

"You do that with beer."

"I know."

"And anyway, Coach says coffee's bad for you."

"Unlike drinking every weekend."

"It stunts your growth."

"You're on the *basketball team*."

"And you can get addicted to caffeine."

"Yeah," I said with another sip, "you see them living under the overpass, caffeine addicts."

"Come *on*! And it tastes gross."

"How do you know? You pour it out. Listen, don't you feel awful tired?"

"Yes, I said already."

137

"Then try this. Extra cream, three sugars, the way I do it."

"What? No. *Black*."

"You don't drink coffee, you just said."

"I still know that. Black, any other way is for girls and fags."

"Ed," I said. "Look at me."

You looked at me, your chin unshaven, hair only sort-of combed, the morning gray and speckled behind you, also beautiful. I tried to sort you out. "You. Must. Stop. With the fag stuff."

"Min—"

"Join the twenty-first century."

"OK, OK, joining."

"Particularly with Al, OK?"

"OK."

"Because he's not."

"OK, I said."

"And people have said that forever about him."

"Then he should stop putting cream in his coffee."

"*Ed.*"

"OK, OK, OK, sorry, sorry, sorry."

"This is complicated enough without you insulting my friend over and over."

"Min—"

"And don't, don't, don't say *no offense*."

"What I was going to say was—what's complicated?"

"You know."

"No. I don't."

"*This.* Me with you, and all the different things. Going to a bonfire, out of place, and now you doing something you don't really want to, just for me. It's like a Portuguese vampire movie."

"What?"

"We're *different*, Ed."

"That's what I keep saying. And I keep saying I like it. I *want* to go here, Min. Just, you know, ten thirty would be fine. I'm tired, is all."

"Really?"

"Yes, *really*. Really, *really* tired. You kept me up late."

With a *shish*, your tires, Joan's tires you were driving, rolled through a puddle. I smiled at you, loved you then, bit my lip to keep from saying it. "But it was worth it," you said.

I kissed you.

"Was that our first fight?"

I kissed you again.

"You taste good."

I laughed. "Well, that's coffee with extra cream and three sugars."

"OK, give me it, if it tastes like it."

I handed it over. You took it and sipped, and then sipped and blinked. Then, a big, big sip.

"I told you."

"Jesus Christ."

"Right?"

"This is—"

"Life-giving brew, is what Al and I call it."

"Fucking delish, I don't care it's a faggy word, oops, sorry, no offense, sorry again. *Delish! Criminy!* This is like a cookie, it tastes like a cookie having sex with a doughnut."

"Wait till the caffeine hits."

"I'm going to have this every morning of my life, and I'm going to shout *Min was right and I was wrong!* when I do."

You actually shouted it. I wonder if you say that every morning now, Ed. I mean I don't wonder, I know you don't, but I hope you think it as you don't. Do you? Don't you?

"So," you said, nodding as I pointed the turn, "did you buy Al life-breathing brew when you took him to this crazy place?"

"Life-*giving*. Probably. We'd been up all night, the only way to get Al up at this hour."

"The only way to get *anyone* up. What did you do all night?"

"Actually, he took me to an orgy."

Your turn signal: *blinka blinka blinka.*

"You're kidding, right?"

"I mostly slept with girls there. A large pile of naked girls all having sex at an orgy. Of course, I know you don't like to think about that, because you're homophobic."

"OK, you're kidding."

"And Al slept with all your girlfriends, and they all said they liked him better."

You swatted me, and I shrieked at the small splash of coffee that landed on my collar. It never came out.

"You know," you said, "I'm not always sure if you're kidding or if you're mad at me or anything."

"I know, Ed."

"I didn't know girls, or anyone, talked this way. Is that why—is that what you meant, complicated?"

I ruffled your hair. The coffee was warm, soaking through to my neck. But I didn't worry on it. You liked how it tasted. "I didn't mean anything," I said. "I was just tired, too."

"Not now, though."

"No," I said, with another sip.

"Me neither."

"That's the caffeine."

You put the car in park and shook your head. "No," you said, "or not just that."

"No?"

Your head kept shaking. "I think it's something else."

It was, Ed. We dashed across the street to Tip Top Goods, the umbrella tucked under my arm because I couldn't hold it up and my coffee cup and your hand too. It was open, the nine stained-glass lamps in a row on the shiny red Chinese bench, lined up in the window, were blazing their colored fringy light to us for once, the usual sign of TIP TOP GOODS OPEN SATURDAYS 7:30–9 AM ONLY NO EXCEPTIONS gone and OPEN BELIEVE IT OR NOT instead. Inside it was a palace, Ed, all the parasols and taxidermy on the ceiling, the mannequins dressed like gypsies sitting on the opium bed writing antique postcards with pricey fountain pens, the rugs on the walls, the wallpaper on the floors, the owner spacing out with his hookah and his black beret, grinning at nothing, and right when we walked in, still laughing, this tome on a stack of silver trays, *Real Recipes from Tinseltown*. Like fate, was the feeling I had as I stood beaming breathless in the shop with this in my hands. Now, of course I see it differently, that it was not fate but *fatal*, fatal and wrong that we read the recipe and got excited and I shared with you all my dreamy plans. Outside it cleared up, as sudden and magic as a vampiric Portuguese sunrise with plumed birds and harps on the sound track. It didn't last, it wasn't clear for much longer, and that's why we broke up, but when I close this book to give it to you, I don't think about that, just us holding the book in our hands to buy it and take it here with us, because damn it Ed, that's not why we broke up. I love it, I miss it, I hate to give it back to you, this complicated thing, it's why we stayed together.

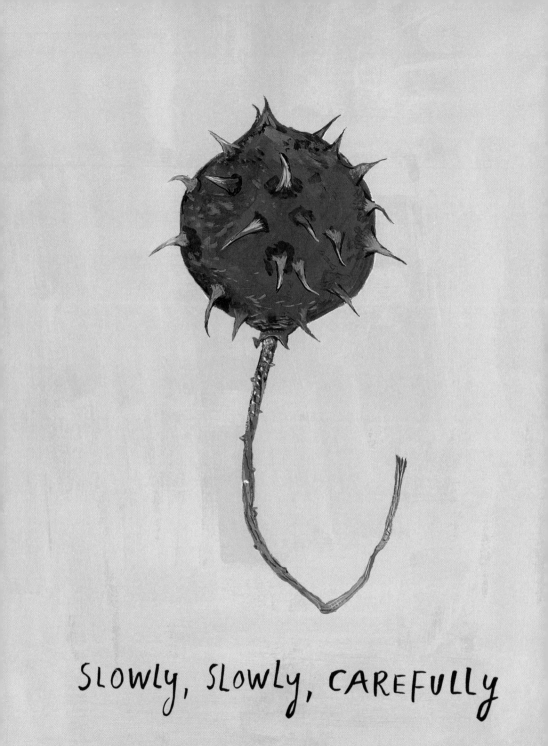

SLOWLY, SLOWLY, CAREFULLY

The sun blinked at us and we blinked back. Outside smelled like perfect leaves, the air clean and breathy, so we crossed to Boris Vian Park and looked at what we had. It was a magical thing, early enough for the park to hold a hush, the mood still and strange like *With My Own Two Eyes*, the scene where Peter Klay flees the identical twin inspectors who have been questioning him and hides behind the statue of some military victory, a winged woman on a horse, and a rustle comes from the bushes and slowly, slowly, carefully, a unicorn emerges and walks in a hushed calm across the misty lawn, and the story of the movie moves to some stranger place. I had that feeling in Boris Vian Park, that anything might happen.

The benches were too wet, even after you did this loopy, chivalrous thing, sitting down and a ridiculous shimmy-slide all the way down, trying to dry it off with your cute butt in jeans, the caffeine from your first real coffee jolting through your body and making me laugh like a baby at bubbles. But even then I wouldn't sit down, it was still too damp, so we soaked our shoes down the slope to the long curve of a weeping willow. I had a feeling. I parted our way through like you do—*did*—with my hair sometimes, and there we were, in a small green space dry and shielded from the rain. We slipped inside and knelt on the ground, all dried leaves and brown grass because nothing got through, just the sun shading down through the branches to keep us safe and hidden.

"Wow."

"Yeah," you said.

"This is the perfect place," I said, "and the perfect thing. It's *perfect*, Ed."

You looked up at the light all around and then at me, very long, until I felt blushy. "It is," you said. "Now tell me why."

"You don't know—? But you just—we just spent fifty-five dollars on this book."

"I know," you said. "It's OK."

146

"But you don't know why?"

You were still looking at me, your hands trembling around the coffee. "To make you happy," you said simply, and my breath was suddenly gone, Ed, with what you said. My hands stayed on the book, which I'd been jumping to open, now frozen with the joy of hearing you and not wanting you to stop. "Min, you know what I'm usually doing now?"

"What?"

"On weekends, I mean."

"This time Saturdays I bet you're usually asleep."

"Min."

"I don't know."

You gave a tremendous shrug, slow, like you were showing me how confusion works. "I don't really, either," you said. "A movie maybe, hanging out somewhere. Somebody's porch with a keg at night. And games, bonfires. It's nothing."

"I like movies."

But you shook your head. "Not these kind, but it's not that. I'm not, I don't know how to say it. When Annette says, she says to me, *So how is this girl different?*, the answer is always long, because it's a long story."

"I'm a long story."

"Not like in English. I was trying to say it in the car, before. It's just—look where I am. I've never been anything, anywhere like this with Jillian, or Amy, or Brianna, Robin—"

"Don't say the whole parade of blondes and whatnot."

"Whatnot." You looked up through the tree, the last couple raindrops tiny stars on the way to evaporating and disappearing. "It's different," you said. "You've made, Min, everything different for me. Everything's like coffee you made me try, better than I ever—or the places I didn't even know were right on the street, you know? I'm like this thing I saw when I was little, where a kid hears a noise under his bed and there's a ladder there that's never been there before, and he climbs down and, it's for kids I know, but this song starts playing. . . ." Your eyes were traveling in the treey light.

"Martin Garner directed that," I said quietly.

"Min, I'd spend fifty-five dollars on anything for you."

I kissed you.

"And ask Trevor, that's like a very big thing, for me, to say *anything* like that."

Again, again.

"So tell me, Min, what did I spend the money on?"

I scooted over to open the book, *Real Recipes from Tinseltown.* "Remember the lobby card you gave me?"

"I don't know what a lobby card is."

I put my hand on your knee, *jiggle jiggle jiggle.*

"Sorry, it's the coffee."

"I know. Lobby cards are, the picture of Lottie Carson you took from the theater."

"That picture I swiped?"

148

"They're not just pictures. On the back is stuff about the star sometimes, all their movies, awards they won if they won any. And, this is what I'm trying to say, *date of birth*."

You put your hand on mine, and we moved together to my leg, jittery too. "I don't get it."

"Ed, I want to have a party."

"What?"

"On December fifth, Lottie Carson is turning eighty-nine."

You didn't say anything.

"I want to have a party for it. For *her*. We can invite her, we followed her to where she lives, we know her address, to send the invitation."

"Invitation," you said.

"Yes," I said, "you know, to invite people."

"I've never had a party like that," you said.

"Don't say it's gay."

"OK, but I don't think I can—"

"We're doing it *together*, Ed. First off we'll have to figure out where to have it. My mom hates me to have parties, plus it should be somewhere glittery, you know, glamorous. Music is easy, Al and I have some thirties music."

"Joan, too," you offered.

"We could do all jazz, that way it will all feel glamorous, even if it's not accurate. Champagne if we can get it."

"Trevor can get anything."

"Trevor would do it for something like this?"

"If I tell him to."

"And you'd tell him to?"

"For you?"

"For the party."

"For this party of yours, yes, OK. And then what's the book for?"

"The fifty-five-dollar book?"

"The fifty-five-dollar book, yes."

I touched you. "The fifty-five-dollar book you bought for me?"

"Min, I'm happy to buy you things, but stop with the fifty-five-dollar part, it's giving me a heart attack."

"OK, well, I was looking through it while you were silly futzing with that samurai sword—"

"Which was *cool.*"

"—and it's *perfect.* I mean, look at the typeface they use here. *Appetizers.*"

"I don't know what typeface is."

"Font."

"OK."

"OK, so the whole book has recipes from movie stars. And look what I opened to, first thing."

"It looks like an igloo."

"It *is* an igloo. It's Will Ringer's recipe, Greta's Cubed-Egg Igloo, inspired by *Greta in the Wild!*"

"That's—"

"—our first date, right. The movie we saw."

You held my face instead of a kiss. It was so still in there, except for your breath, sour and coffee-quick. "So we're going to make that crazy thing?"

"Not just that," I said, and flipped pages. "Look at this."

"Oh."

"Yeah, wow, right? Lottie Carson's Stolen-Sugar Pensieri Sweets. These delectables, says America's Cinematic Lovely, were born from necessity, growing up as she did with not two dimes to rub together. 'My mother, bless her heart, would do anything to keep the nine of us fed and happy, and when times were tight, she'd snitch sugar from Mrs. Gunderson's bridge club. The old bat hired her to clean up after their get-togethers, and my mother would empty the sugar bowl into her purse, go to Saint Boniface's and confess, and then whip up a batch of these, waiting piping hot when we got home from school. The icing is made with Pensieri, a liqueur Poppa allowed himself every Friday. Father, forgive me—these just don't taste as snappy if the sugar's not stolen!'"

Your grin was wicked and cute. "So we're going to steal sugar," you said.

"Will you? Can we?"

"Sure, there's that diner near here. Lopsided's. But it's in those big things."

I looked us over. "Thrifty Thrift should have a coat, like an overcoat for five dollars. I'll buy *that* for you, with nice deep pockets. You need another coat anyway, Ed. You can't dress up like a basketball player every day in that jacket."

"I *am* a basketball player."

"But today you're a sugar thief."

"We steal the sugar to make the cookies," counting on your fingers in your arithmetic voice, "and get Trevor to get champagne, and you and Joan and Al for music."

"The igloo," I said.

"The igloo," you said, "and figure out where to have it, and send invitations to this movie star we followed."

"December fifth. Tell me, *please* tell me that it's not a game day."

You brushed hair from my face. I kissed you and stopped to look at your mouth. It was little, it was not sure of itself, but it was a smile. "You do know," you said, "that we don't know for sure it's her, so it's crazy to—"

"But we think so, right?"

"Yes," you said.

"Yes," I said, "and even if it isn't—"

"Even if it isn't?"

"Maybe that date's familiar to you. December fifth."

You bit your lip strange and blew down at the leafy ground. "Min, you told me your birthday, I swear to God I hope I'm remembering, isn't until—"

"It's our two-month anniversary."

"What?"

"It will be, that's all. Two months from *Greta in*—"

"You think about things like that already?"

"Yes."

"All the time?"

"Ed, no."

"But sometimes?"

"Sometimes."

You sighed very deeply.

"I shouldn't have said that," I said quickly. "Are you— you're freaking out."

"I'm freaking out," you said, if you remember, because something tells me that you might have decided to remember it differently, "I'm freaking out that I'm not freaking out."

"Really?"

I lost my breath again, with how you smiled. "Yes."

"Should we go?"

"OK, to steal sugar. Oh, wait, to the coat place."

"Shit, Thrifty Thrift doesn't open until ten. I learned the hard way. We need to wait."

Now, you kissed me in this great place with a confidence, a joy, with no shrug, hungrily, eager. "Gosh," you said, your eyes blinky with pretend wonder, putting down your coffee as far from us as you could reach, "I wonder what me and my girlfriend can do for an hour or so in a hidden part of the park?"

Clark Baker couldn't have said it better. This was the first time we were both naked, our clothes in separate piles and us sitting together, so close that in a shot from above, the light basking and trickling down to us through the goosepimply breeze, you might not know, not see, whose hand was whose was where. You looked so gorgeous naked in the lovely lilty green light, like some creature not quite from Earth, even with a few smudges of mud on your legs, particularly afterward, your chest heaving slower and slower with a little sweat, or maybe just damp from my mouth, on the small of your back, your hands cupped together bashful between your legs until I made you move them so I could see and start all over again. And me, I never felt so beautiful, in the light and in your arms almost crying. Two last sips of your cold coffee and we got dressed to go, trying to brush off what we could, socks reluctant to unroll, my bra cold at the underwire, my shirt, my coat. But I was warmer now, from the brightening sun and from everything, so I just wadded up my cardigan and held it under my arm as we left Boris Vian Park with the guy with the stroller wondering where we'd come from, and left it in your sister's car the rest of the day, so not until I was home stomping upstairs, yelling back bored at my mother, did I toss it onto the bed and see this bounce from someplace onto my floor, and I picked it up and flushed thinking of how it got mixed in with my things. I put it in my drawer, whatever it is, and then in the box, and now it's for you to flush and regret about. Who knows, a seed of some kind, a fruit, a pod, a unicorn loping through the underbrush where we lay together. Put it in water, I could have done, taken care of it and who knows what might have grown, what might have happened with this thing from the park where I loved you, Ed, so much.

And here's the coat I bought you, so happy to spend the eight dollars. "Let's see what we can hide in it," you said, and pulled me to you, and we giggled as you buttoned up around us both, kissing me cocooned against you, and you tried to walk that way to the cash register, a stride like a vaudeville hobo, with me kissing you and leaning my head back until I thought the buttons would burst, and I unpeeled away to open my purse and look at you, look at you, Ed.

So—fucking—beautiful.

"Will you wear it to school?"

"Not a chance," you laughed.

"*Please.* Look at the pattern. You can tell people I made you do it."

"After the sugar caper I never want to see it again."

Here it is, Ed. Nor I, you.

Some of the sugar has spilled and scattered at the bottom of the box. The opposite of how I feel, everything in here tinged with sugar. But, let's face it, it went without a hitch. Lopsided's served us breakfast, fruit and toast for me, two eggs with bacon, sausage and hash browns and a short stack of hotcakes and a large orange juice for you, coffee with extra cream and a three-sugar pour from the dispenser for both of us. We talked a little and I paged through the recipes, waiting for you to finish and to wipe your mouth, which finally I had to do myself. Here and there I felt leaf bits and blades of grass on my skin, my clothes pressing them in deeper like a ceramics project I did once. In the bath-room mirror there was even a smudge of dirt on my neck, and I wiped it off in a hurried flush, the cheap paper towel so rough against my skin that I looked for a scrape in my reflection and then, meeting my own eyes, stood for a sec and tried to figure, like all girls in all mirrors everywhere, the difference between lover and slut. EMPLOYEES MUST WASH HANDS was the answer. Back at the booth the other diners ignored us, or looked at us in envy or admiration or disgust, or there weren't any other diners there, I don't know. To stop staring at you, I kept fiddling with the sugar until you stopped my hand with yours.

"Isn't that like visiting the scene of the crime?"

"The crime hasn't happened yet," I said.

"Still," you said, "maybe don't call attention to the sugar that's about to vanish."

I stopped. "I'm a virgin."

You almost spat out orange juice. "OK."

"I just thought I'd tell you."

"OK."

"Because I didn't before."

"Listen, it's OK." You coughed a little. "Some of my best friends are virgins."

"Really?"

"Hmm. No. I guess not anymore."

"*All* my friends are virgins," I said.

"Oh!" you said. "There's Bill Haberly, shit, wasn't supposed to tell anybody."

"See, the fact that that's remarkable—"

"No, no. I've known, you know, lots of virgins."

"So they weren't virgins after you met them, is what you're saying."

You went bright red. "I didn't say that, that's none of your business, wait, you were teasing, right? Kidding?"

"I guess it turns out I wasn't."

"Look, it's hard for me to talk about this stuff like you can."

"Are you surprised?"

"That you're talking about it, yeah."

"No, that I'm—"

"Yeah. I guess. I mean, you had that boyfriend last year, right? John, that guy."

"Joe."

"Yeah."

"You knew that?" What I meant was, Ed, you were looking at me then?

"Annette told me, actually. So I guess I was surprised."

"Well. No. We didn't."

"OK. That's OK."

"I mean, we wanted to. I mean, he did. We both did, I wasn't sure."

"It's OK."

"Yeah?

"Yes, what did you think? That I'm some—asshole?"

"No, I don't know. I just, it's because it's the same again."

"What is?"

"I'm not sure, I mean."

"Whoa, we don't have to."

"No?"

"No," you said. "This is, like, *early*, you know? Isn't it?"

"For me, but you have a different thing. I mean, your crowd, the bonfires and everything."

"It's all talk at a bonfire. Mostly, anyway."

"OK."

"Wait, are you saying what we—in the park, or, you know, last night—you didn't want to—?"

"No, no."

"No? You didn't—?"

"*No,*" I said. "*Yes.* I just wanted to tell you what I told you."

"OK."

"Because I didn't before, like I said."

"OK," you said, but then you knew that was wrong. You tried, "Thank you?"

And I almost said I love you. Instead I said nothing and you said nothing. The waitress came to refill us and left the check. We split it and then, with the pile of bills on the little tray, looked at each other. Maybe you were just feeling buzzy and full, but I was feeling—*happy*. Grateful, I guess, and light. Lovely even, plus the new coffee shivery inside me. And I almost said it again. Instead—

"Now."

"What?"

I leaned forward to you, your forehead warm against mine. "The sugar," I whispered. *"Now."*

But Ed, you'd taken it already.

This is one of those things, Ed, where you're not going to know what the hell it is. "This really is different," Joan said when we walked in, although I couldn't tell you how she said it, pleased but also suspicious somewhere in there. The kitchen was oniony, Hawk Davies on again. "You asked to borrow the car, and you're back before you usually get up. What are you two, smugglers?"

You didn't answer her but plunked down the sugar on the counter, next to a towel where hoop earrings, it looked like, were set out to dry or cool.

"And what's that coat?" Joan asked. "It looks—"

"Min bought it for me."

"—dapper."

"Good save, sis. I need a shower. Back in a minute."

"Your towel," she called to you already bounding up, "is on the floor where you left it from your shower four hours ago that *woke me up!*"

"You know what you're not," you replied in a yawn. A door slammed. Joan looked at me, brushed hair out of her eyes as the water went on upstairs. I'm here again, is what I thought.

"What about you, Min?" she asked. "Do *you* need a shower?"

"I'm good," I said. There was a vibration in the kitchen, Ed, that you left me alone with, that I wasn't catching.

"Are you," she mused. "You always look like a rabbit in the headlights when he goes upstairs. Come in, come in, tell me what's on your mind."

I leaned against the counter. Onion rings, they were, and Joan plucked them one by one to mix into a big bowl of noodles and basil and tofu.

"Vermicelli?" she offered.

"We just came from Lopsided's."

"So I see. Isn't diner theft a little freshman year?"

I held up the book and started to explain. Your sister munched over my shoulder, tilting her head a little when she wanted me to turn the page because her fingers were a little lime-juicy. She didn't say anything, just kept chopstick-ing her lunch or breakfast, so I kept saying things—Lottie Carson, *Greta in the Wild*, eighty-ninth birthday. Her eyes widened, and closed in slow blinks, but still she didn't say anything, so I told her everything, Ed, everything except two-month anniversary and fifty-five dollars.

"Wow," she said finally.

"Cool, huh?"

"I really should lend you my film books," she said, and put her bowl in the sink.

"That'd be cool," I said, "and Hawk Davies too."

"I like how you think," Joan said, and then looked at me very seriously, waiting.

"Thank you?" I said.

"And my brother," she nodded at the stairs you'd run up, "is going to help you make these fancy foods for a film star's birthday?"

"Do you think it's," I said, "I don't know."

She grabbed two apricots, gave me one. "Think it's what?" she said gently. "Crazy?"

"Possible, I was going to say, feasible."

She sighed. The apricot was juicy, and I put down the book, open at Lottie Carson's smile, and wiped my hands. "It might be complicated, Min."

"Yeah, the igloo's crazy, right? I mean where do you even get—"

She said that wasn't what she meant, and the kitchen felt so strange that I just pushed on through, kept talking, and threw the pit in the trash. I had a feeling, but I did not know what it was. "The cookies seem easier."

The shower turned off. She sighed again and looked at the recipe. "Yeah, pretty straightforward. Where are you going to get what is it, Pensieri?"

"I have a plan," I said, shrugging at the ceiling where you were drying off. "Somehow I'll do it, and soon."

"Maybe tonight?" she said. "Did Ed tell you? He can't hang out tonight, he has a family thing."

"He did not," I said, "tell me."

Hawk Davies ended. "Yeah," she said carefully, "that sounds like him not to tell you," and I did not know what was going on that I was feeling. She was looking at me in a delicate way I guess, like I'd used some word wrong and she was afraid to tell me, or like I was the basketball star and it was her brother the virgin up in his room, like she was protecting something. My hand felt grippy, my eyes hot.

"Should I go?" I managed to say.

Joan exhaled and touched my shoulder. "Don't say it like that, Min. We just have, a thing I said, a family thing tonight. We have to get ready for it before too long." With a little clamor, she put a few things in the dishwasher, nudged it closed with her slipper, picked up a bright blue sponge. She was surprised, I remembered, that we had come back so early. Now it was almost too late. "You must be tired anyway, huh? You were up almost as late as he was."

Was that it, is what I thought. That I'd kept you up too late? But she didn't say anything more.

"Let me just say good-bye," I said, and she said, "Of course of course," and I bounded up the stairs, the cushions in the living room, I noticed, back on the sofa. Your mom's door closed again like always. Your room I'd only seen for minutes at a time, the ugly dresser, basketball guys on the wall, a shelf of the books people gave you who didn't know, or knew but hoped not, you'd never read. Protractor, other geeky math whatnot on the also-ugly desk, crowded with crap and dirty plates. The radio muttering, shades still down, sweaty sweaty smell, mostly disgusting but not, what's wrong with me, entirely disgusting, no.

You were in bed so perfect that at first I thought you were doing it for a joke, playing possum asleep with the towel around you slipping a little, your leg bent at the knee and your arm over your face like you were hiding a smile. But then you snored like nobody would pretend, and I stood in the doorway watching you sleep. I waited just to see you at that kind of peace, I wanted to be beside you, I wanted you to wake up slowly or startle, or just half awaken and turn over and go back to sleep or murmur my name. I wanted to watch you forever, or sleep beside you forever, or sleep forever while you woke and watched me, something forever anyway. I wanted to kiss you, rumple your hair, rest three fingertips on your hip bone warm and smooth, wake you that way or hush you back to sleep. To see you naked at rest, to cover you with a blanket, there's not enough ink and paper to say all I wanted. But I couldn't stay long, so I just went back downstairs where Joan was waiting with a kind smile. "He's asleep," I said.

"You wore him out with your adventures," she said, handing me the sugar and books. "See you soon, Min."

"I didn't leave him a note or anything," I said.

"Good," she said with a snort. "He hates reading."

"But tell him to call me."

"I'll tell him."

"Keep the sugar."

"No, Min, take it home. Otherwise *I'll* cook with it and you'll have to steal more and you'll end up in the big house and it'll all be my fault."

That made me smile, *the big house*. "But you'd break me out, right?" I said. "You'd lend Ed the car again for a getaway? Oh, wait, my sweater's in the car."

We walked out together into the drizzle, and she unlocked the car and handed the sweater to me. Now I had quite a pile in my hands, far from home with nobody to help me carry anything. "See you, Min."

"Bye," I said. It was strange and wet, burdened like that, with Joan already stepping fast back to your back door.

"Thanks for the book," though I wanted to say, for some reason, *Sorry*.

She shut the door. Alone on the bus, all my items on the seat next to me like an inventory, the cookbook more expensive now looking at it by myself, less charming. And clenched in my hand I found this towel, the oil from the onion rings in permanent circles on the cloth. I kept it instead of giving it back to Joan the next time I visited, because I don't know why. Each of those things she made waiting for her brother, each one crunchy and unburned, feasible as can be, I can see it. Her elegant life, the way she cared for people in her house. And those traces on the towel I stared at on the way home to sit quietly, friends for once, with my mother, Earl Grey tea, toast. Wanting to cry a little bit, folding the towel to keep it in the box, not knowing if those circles looked wide open, a laughing mouth, a bright moon, a rising bubble, or just how I see it now, a square of zeros in invisible ink from the kitchen. I thought it was one thing but it was the other, it was zero zero zero alone on the bus, while you slept in the room I had to leave, and that's why we broke up.

And my umbrella, lost that day, where is it? I know I had it that morning. Give it back, Ed if you have it, I'm lost without it on rainy days, although it's December now, so it's they say snow, and an umbrella in a snowstorm is ridiculous, a seat belt if you're not in a car, a helmet if you're not on a bike, like a fish needs a bicycle or however they say it, like coffee needs to be black, like a virgin needs a boyfriend. So many things I'll never get back.

By now I'm sure you are wondering, how long does it take to get to you? Is Al driving his father's shop's truck to Bolivia and then turning around and coming back, all these pages for a simple trip, even in traffic? And the answer, Ed, is Leopardi's. I never took you to Leopardi's, which is my first-favorite coffee place, the best one, a crumbling Italian palace with bright red walls unpeeling their paint and photographs hung crooked of dark-skinned men with their hair in great slick stylish curves and the kindhearted smirks they give to their mistresses and an espresso machine like a shiny mad-scientist castle, steaming and gleaming and spouts everywhere curving down and out in a writhing metallic nest underneath a stern brass eagle perched on top like it's looking for prey. It takes that whole machine, dials and releases and a stack of square white towels the staff uses expertly, to make tiny, tiny cups of coffee as deep and dark as the first three Malero films that make the world angled and blinky. Goddamn I love that coffee. If I put in extra cream, three sugars, the eagle would fly down and talon my throat open before I had a sip, but you know what, Ed? That's not the real magic of the place, the Leopardi's enchantment from the first time Al showed it to me when his cousin worked there when we were in eighth grade. It's the utter silence of the tall room, the thinky meditation uninterrupted by anything but great hissing clouds of steam and the jangling change on the counter. They leave you alone, they let you mutter or laugh or read or argue or whatnot in any corner where you're sitting. They don't clear your table, they don't clear their throats, they don't say a word to you except *prego*, you're welcome, if you say thank you, *grazie*. They don't notice or they pretend not to notice, even if you finish the last drips of your coffee and then slam down your cup at something your ex-boyfriend did, just the thought of it. You can crack the saucer in half, but they don't say anything. They figure, at Leopardi's, you have trouble enough. They should teach my mother, everybody's mother, how to leave people alone. It was the perfect place Al could take me, when we were getting close to your house with this letter nowhere near done, lugging the box in here with no Leopardi's man with their perfect mustaches and aprons saying a word about the thunk of the box at the neighboring table or how long I've been sitting here writing to you.

This is the bottle of Pensieri. I never told you about Leopardi's, and I never told you about the night I had getting Pensieri, just this one bottle, you never asked, while you had—ha!—your *family thing*. I never told you. There's a lot, Ed, I never told you. Let me tell you some of it.

It was late afternoon, enough tea enough Mom, when I finally showered Boris Vian Park off me and sat in my own room like I hadn't been there in a hundred years, my backpack still unzipped from Friday, the pennant still curled up on my desk from the game. I picked up a few things, still in my towel, scrubbed at the coffee on my collar and left it to drip hopefully on the shower rod, put some music on and turned it off, it all sounded wrong, Hawk Davies was all I wanted and didn't have. Then I did what I was embarrassed to do, which was pick up the phone and call Al, slumped back down on the bed while it rang, flipped open *When the Lights Go Down: A Short Illustrated History of Film.*

"Hello?"

"If there is a film that with more elegance and imagination strikes more deeply into the fierce and tender truths of the human heart," I said, "it has yet to be unearthed by this humble critic."

Al's sigh crackled the receiver. "Hey, Min."

"*Two Pairs of Shoes*, blandly ignored upon its release, belittled and dismissed even at times by the director, has gradually emerged like a volcanic island rising from the ocean to take its proper place as a powerful landmark on the horizon of film history."

"Please tell me you're reading out loud from something, because otherwise it's overboard even for you."

"*When the Lights Go Down: A Short Illustrated History of Film*. Let's see it tonight."

"What?"

"*Two Pairs of Shoes*. Come on, I'll stop at Limelight and find it. All you'll have to do is popcorn and put some pants on."

Al told me once late at night that usually when we're talking on the phone, he's pacing around his room in his boxers. We made a deal one morning early when he couldn't pay attention that I'd never tell anyone if I could tease him mercilessly about it forever. "Min, do you know what time it is?"

"Four thirty."

"Quarter of five," he said, "*Saturday*. You're calling to make plans Saturday night when Saturday night's already started."

"Don't be cranky like you are sometimes."

"I don't like you when you assume that I don't have anything to do. I don't mope around while you go out boy-friending."

Al gets like this sometimes. Another word from our vocab flash cards, *petulant*. I can handle it, though. "Al, *I'm* the one with no plans. Let's watch a movie or please please let me tag along with whatever you've got."

"What did Ed do?"

"What?"

"What did he do to you?"

My body flushed a little remembering the weeping willow. I never tell Al that I'm often in a towel talking to him. "Nothing, he just has a family thing."

"You told me you had a busy weekend."

"Al, *please*. I have nothing. Whatever you're doing, bring me along. Monster truck show, inventory at your dad's, make-out session with Christine Edelman, *anything*."

That made him laugh. You've probably never noticed Christine Edelman, she's in our lit class and looks like a professional wrestler.

"I'm free," Al admitted. "I have nothing, I'm the usual loser."

"You just wanted to make me suffer."

"What's the use of friendship?" he said, our version of *What are friends for?*

"Great, I'll bring the movie."

"I'll sneak Christine out the back."

"Ew."

"Why do you think I'm in my boxers?"

"Ew!"

I never told you any of this, Ed. You never asked me what I did that night or how I managed to get Pensieri. I never told you that Al had not just popcorn but polenta with lamb chops and asparagus ready to broil in case I hadn't eaten, which I hadn't, and a spot, just a spot near his ear, of cream, like he'd just shaved minutes before. I had the movie and bad clothes on.

"Hey," I said walking in. "What's this on?"

"Mark Clime," he said. "*Live at the Blue Room*. It's my mom's."

"I like it," I said. "It has the same kind of feel—did I tell you about this guy I've been listening to, Hawk Davies? I really like him."

Al gave me a funny smile. "Yeah, you told me, Min."

"Oh, right. Ed's sister—"

"Joan."

"Joan, she told me. She'll lend it to me she says, soon. I'll copy it for you too."

"OK. So, how was his game?"

"What?"

"Basketball. Your boyfriend plays."

"Oh, I know, I know. OK, actually."

"Really?" Al was making this thing we like, mashing up mint and this Italian lemon syrup that comes in a round glass lemon bottle at the bottom of a tall glass, then ice and imported fizzy Italian water his parents have in the house like most people have milk.

"Well, no," I said. God, that drink is good. We can never decide what to call it. "It was boring and loud. I can tell you that, right?"

"You can tell me anything."

"Well, it was boring. But Ed was nice, and even the bonfire, and after, was nice."

"After?"

"Um," I said, and took a long sip, the ice slapping around my nose a little. I had a sudden question in my head there wasn't room for, a question about you, Ed. Al had just said it, *You can tell me anything*, and was waiting for me to say something, opening the oven to peek on the food for no reason, the lamb and asparagus waiting in their beds with the lights on. But I couldn't ask it. I couldn't live the life of those Japanese directors who can take a long, long time to show a flower on the screen, a drop of water on a smooth black table going nowhere, a spiderweb lit by the moon that's nothing to do with the plot, the image there for no reason except they liked it, and liked it not fitting. My question didn't belong in Al's loyal kitchen with my friend wiping his hand on the towel tucked into his belt like always, so I just looked down at his shoes with my eyes closed like I just loved the music, until Al asked me if I was OK, and I opened my eyes brightly, brightly, brightly and said yes, of course I was OK. We got plates and sat to watch.

A girl meets a boy, Ed, and everything changes, or so she says. She walks down the street and the storefronts look the same, even as we linger on their flickering reflections. The cars move quickly, slowly, quickly down the block. She gets coffee and says it tastes different, quietly, to herself. The sky looks sad, she says, but she's not sad. It rains and she sees the boy again. The phone rings—it's another day, or the same day, who can tell, the girl thinks with her coffee, when the whole world has changed? She gets coffee again, the cars go by, reflected in the window. The world, she thinks, has changed.

"Min, I don't get this at all. What's with the store window they keep showing? When is something going to happen?"

"You don't like it," I said. "We can turn it off if you want."

"I have no opinion of it."

"*Al.*"

"I don't! I just don't get it is all."

"*Cinéma du moment*, they call it. Cinema of the moment. You don't like it."

"Don't put this on me, Min. *You* don't like it and want

184

to turn it off, but you feel weird about it because of some book, *When the Dark*—"

"*When the Lights Go Down.* That's not why I feel weird about it."

"Then you feel weird about it for the same reason I do, because for forty minutes we've watched this French girl wandering around thinking things. Look, the cars are going by again. Are you sure this is the right movie?"

"*Two Pairs of Shoes.*"

"I don't get it."

"You don't like it."

"I have no opinion."

I turned it off, the crappy movie. This is how we were, Ed, me and Al. You never got it and I never really told you how it was, *old married couple,* Al's mom called it once and just laughed when Al said, "Well, Mamma, you should know." I looked at him, I never told you this Ed, him stacking the plates, the music back on, making me another lemon whatever-it-is. It crackled in the air again, my question, electric around us even if Al didn't know it. I don't know where it came from. They tell you, in the pamphlets they throw at us, they say talk to your parents or a clergyman or a trusted teacher or friend. But there is nobody acceptable on that list, parents part of the problem, a teacher who will say *There are some conversations I'm not really allowed to have with you,* and most friends squealing to their other friends just like a clergyman will tattle to God. So you're left alone, or with the only person, my friend Al, to lay it on. And so you lay it on him, unfair awkward, for no reason except the reason you have to ask the question, so I asked my friend Al, foolish I know, if I could ask him something.

"Sure," clattering the dishes.

"It's kind of personal."

He turned off the water and watched me in the doorway with the towel on his shoulder. "OK."

"I mean, not like my period or my parents beating me, but personal."

"Yeah, it's rough when your parents beat you *and* you have your period."

"*Al.*"

"*Min.*"

"It's about sex."

His house got quiet the way every room does with the word *sex*, even the jazz musicians leaning forward in the hopes of hearing it through the speakers even as they kept playing.

"Beer," Al said, a decision that surprised him. "I need, do you want a beer? My parents have a few Scarpia's, they'll never know."

"*Al*, you know me and beer."

"I know you, I know you." He leaned into the open fridge and took out a bottle, opened it with the towel, tossed

186

the cap—so unlike him—into the kitchen sink. Took a long sip.

"If you don't want to talk about it," I said.

"It's OK," he said, and sat next to me on the sofa. The Scarpia's fizzed, the band played on.

"I can't ask anyone else."

"OK."

"I really can't. And we're friends."

"Yes," he said, with another sip.

"So don't freak out."

"OK."

"Don't."

"OK I said."

"Because I need to ask someone."

"Min, this is turning into that movie with you saying it over and over. Just ask what you—"

"Am I," I asked, "is it OK to not be a virgin?"

Al sat up straight and put the beer on the coffee table. "So, you're telling me—?"

"No," I said. "I am, still."

"Because that would be quick."

"OK," I said. "Maybe you've answered it, I guess."

"Min, I'm just saying."

"No, no, you're right."

"Just a couple *weeks*, right?"

"Yes. But I *didn't*. I *haven't*. But you would think—"

"I would have no opinion, Min."

"Don't say that. You said *quick*."

"Well, it would be."

"*Quick* is an opinion."

"No, Min." Al finished the beer but kept looking at it. "*Quick* is an adjective."

We smiled at each other a little bit. "I guess what I'm asking—"

"I think I know what you're asking. I don't know, Min."

"Is it OK, is what I mean."

"Is it OK not to be a virgin, *yes*. Most people aren't virgins, Min. That's why there's people to begin with."

"Yeah, but—" I jiggled my leg on the sofa. I didn't care about those people, I thought. I just cared about you. "What do you think," I asked, "is what I'm asking. You're a guy."

"Yes."

"So you know how you think about it. If a girl, you know, if you fool around in a car let's say, or a park."

"Jesus, Min. What park?"

"No, no, just if. For example."

"OK, then what kind of car? Because if it was the new M-3—"

I pillow-swatted him. "What do people think about that?"

"People?" Al said.

"*Al*. Different *people*. You know!"

188

"Different people think different things."

"I know, but, like, a *guy*."

"Some guys like it, I guess. I mean, of course. Sexy, right? Some would think worse things. And then, some people would think something else I guess, I don't know, this is ridiculous Min, I have no opinion."

"It's not ridiculous," I said, "not to me. Al, what I'm trying to ask is, what about you?"

Al stood up, so careful and quiet, like he had shattered glass all over him, or was holding a baby. I was stupid, yes, a fool and an idiot. I am an idiot, Ed, it's another reason we broke up. "What about me what?" he said.

"What do you think," I said, "and don't say you have no opinion."

Al looked around the room. The music waited. "I guess I think, Min, that when I think about sex, you know, I want it to feel *good*. Not *feel good*, shut up, but *right*. Happy, not just banging away somewhere. You know, you should not just do it to do it. You should love the guy."

"I do," I said quietly, "love the guy."

Al stood still for a sec. Quietly, quietly he sighed to me, like the way the cookie crumbles. "Not to sound like that movie they made us watch," he said, "but Min, how do you know you're not just—"

"I know what you think he's like," I said, "but he's not like that."

Al shook his head, very hard. "I have no opinion of him. It's just, tell me something, Min, if you're going to tell me. You love him."

"Yes."

"And you told him?"

"I think he knows."

"So you haven't. And has he said anything?"

"Al, no."

"Then how can you—how do you know he's—"

I told him. I never told you this, but I told Al our plans, the things we were planning for the star we followed. I didn't have the cookbook with me, or the lobby card—but he listened to the sugar we stole, the coat I bought you, the recipes perfect for the party. Al didn't want to like it, he didn't want to be excited, but he couldn't help it.

"I know where we could get those egg things, I bet," he said.

"I know, Vintage Kitchen," I said. "I thought that. How many would we need, you think, to make the igloo?"

"It might be expensive," he said. "If you show me the recipe you found—I can't believe you took Ed Slaterton to Tip Top Goods. Is nothing sacred?"

"If you liked getting up early," I said.

"Don't put this on me. And *when* again is this party?"

"December fifth, because Al, can I tell you what it also is? It's our, Ed and I's, two-month anniversary."

Al looked at me again. "That's another thing you didn't tell him, right? *Please* tell me that. Because definitely a guy thing I can tell you, they—*we* don't want to hear that kind of thing, too early, too *quick*. Don't tell a guy two-month anniversary."

"I told him," I said, "and he loves it." An *idiot*.

Al gave me a long, slow blink. "I guess it's love," he said.

"I guess so," I said. "But Al, what do you think?"

"I think I don't want to miss that party," he said. "Do you think she'll really come? I mean, if it's her. It's probably—"

"If we invite her right," I said, "and if it's her. But the thing is, Al, you're our only chance for Pensieri."

"What?"

"For the cookies. You gotta have that in the shop, right? It's weird and Italian."

"So *everything* about the stolen-sugar whatevers will be stolen?"

"Well—"

"Because there's no way my dad's giving us a bottle of that. They're like seventy-something dollars, made from rare baby plums or something."

"Have you ever had it?"

"If I'd had it, Min," Al said, gentle and sighing, "it would have been with you. You're the only one."

"So you'll get it for me? Us?"

Al looked at his watch. "Now would be a good time, actually. We'll take the truck, I have the keys."

"Will you get in trouble?"

"Nah, I do the inventory now. They'll never notice, no-body buys that stuff."

"Thank you, Al."

"Sure."

"No," I said. "I mean, *thank you*. For tonight, all of it."

Al gave that sigh again. "What's," he said, "the use of friendship?"

Ed, I'll tell you what's the use of friendship, because we never were friends. The use is racing off into the night, is what the use is. Rolling down the windows, the rained-out air in our faces all the way to the shop. The use is the good talking, and the not talking as we got there. The use is the fun bicker of what the best robbery movie is as we slipped into the shop and the hilarity at the final right answer, *Catty Cat and the Cat Burglar*, which we saw together in second grade and never forgot, the badly animated cape of Catty Cat, the British voice of villain Doghouse Wiley, the theme song, *Catty Cat, Catty Cat, cape and boots and crazy hat, fighting crime, doin' fine, would you take a look at that?*, singing it down the darkened aisles of the shop, casting the shadows of strange bottles in our path, the imported shapes of oil and pickled whatnot and skyscraper square boxes of pasta, salamis swinging like bats sleeping upside down over the cash register, the green-red-white neon stripes on the clock shining on the baby photo of Al, huge and faded, up on the wall. This is what the use of friendship is, Ed: Al coming down from the stepladder, leaning so close I thought, was afraid for a sec, he would kiss me, sliding this bottle cold and dusty into my hands.

"Thank you, thank you, thank you."

He waved it away, but then, "Can I ask you something?"

"Yeah. *Look* at this label."

"Min, why didn't we ever talk like this before?"

"What do you mean?"

"Well, you went out with Joe for how long, and you never asked me anything about what would a guy think."

"Well, but Joe was like you. *Us.*"

"No, he wasn't. Not to me, anyway."

"You liked him, I thought."

Al put the ladder away. "Min, Joe was a manipulative dick."

"What?"

"Yes."

"You never—"

"I can tell you now."

"You said you had no opinion. When we broke up, that's what you said."

"I know what I said."

"Well, do you know what you're *saying*? I *asked* you

something tonight, and now it's like I don't know if I can trust it, what you told me."

"What?"

"Don't *what?* like that. Al, I'm going out with Ed Slaterton. I think I—I told you I love him and you are my best friend and I want to know you're not a *liar* about it."

"Stop this. You say this when you're holding an expensive bottle I stole from my dad for your scheme?"

"I thought it was *our* scheme," I said. "Al, what do you think of my boyfriend and don't say *no opinion*."

"Don't ask me then. Because I don't know him."

"Don't lie to me. You don't like him."

"I don't know him."

"It was him tearing down that poster, right? It was just a poster, Al."

"Min."

"Or the jukebox at Cheese Parlor, but you can't blame him for that, because you guys, Lauren especially, were totally—"

"Min, *no.*"

"Then what?"

"What what?"

"What," I said firmly, "do you think of him?"

"Don't ask me."

"I am asking you."

And Ed, I never told you what he said. He didn't say he had no opinion. He had an opinion.

The night broke apart then, and I never told you about it, and now it's scarcely something I can put in order— shouting outside the shop, knocking over one of the displays, Al's insistence, the way he gets when he decides this time he will not be, not be, not! Be! Wrong! Crying on the bus, realizing it was the wrong bus goddamnit, Al calling after me in the parking lot not to be an idiot. Me, being an idiot, slamming into the house, waking up my mother. Al mad and silent, the door of the shop open and the lights on to clean up the mess. Nothing like a movie, nothing I like, telling my stupid mother I was with *Al* and that she doesn't have to fucking worry about that anymore, it would never, never happen again. Asleep. Crying. Throwing my clothes off, putting the bottle carefully in the drawer, it not fitting in the drawer, getting a box from the basement. Shrieking *"Nothing!"* at my mother, crying. Slamming the basement door, wiping my nose. I never told you any of this. Emptying the drawer into the box, muttering out loud to myself. Asleep, crying again, a bad dream. And then the phone ringing in the morning and it was you, Ed.

"Min, I tried to call you before."

"What?"

"Last night. But I couldn't—it just rang, so I hung up."

"I was with a friend."

"Oh."

I sighed. "Or maybe—"

"Joan's gone." You sounded hoarse. "She'll be gone all day and my mom's at the Center and I want to talk to you. Can you come over?"

I swear I was walking in your door before I hung up the phone, looking at you. You looked a wreck, your eyes angry and unslept. I put the Pensieri down on the table, but you didn't even look at it, circling around like you were on the court, kitchen-hallway-living room-kitchen, sweaty. I felt crazed to see you, each glimpse of your eyes a reply, a new win of the argument against Al, my mother, anybody in the whole world, all the liars, everybody and everyone.

"Listen," you said, "I want to say sorry about what Joan did. I couldn't believe it when I woke up and you were gone."

I'd almost forgotten about it, sort of. "That's OK."

You slapped a bookcase. "No, it isn't. She shouldn't have done that shit."

"You had a family thing, it's OK."

"Ha!" Ed said. I couldn't help it, it made me giggle. You gave me a grin, surprised, a sharp smile, and said it again. "Ha!"

"Ha!"

"*Ha!* You want to know what a *family thing* is, for Joan? It's, she wants to talk to me, so she sends my friends away. It's such bullshit, a family thing. My mom is who she got it from, but it's not working, she's not my mom." You looked scared, for some reason, to say that, a look I'd seen you get at practice when Coach blew the whistle and you thought maybe you'd screwed up and you were in trouble.

"It's OK," I said.

"I mean, she could have waited, you know, to talk to me. But of course she couldn't, because she's *out all day today!* With *Andrea!* But if it's *my* girlfriend, then throw her out of the house because we have to talk right this minute!"

"What did she want to talk to you about?"

You stopped pacing and sat down real sudden on a chair in the corner. And then got up, almost comical, like a Piko and Son movie, except you weren't switching hats with anybody. "Listen," you said. "I want to tell you something."

"OK." This was about your mom, I decided, wrong again Ed, wrong always is what I idiot am.

"What she wanted to say was that with you I was, that we're going too fast is what she said. You told her about the movie-star thing and she knew I'm not like that and she said it was one thing with, like, the other girls I go out with, before. But that you were so smart and like, I don't know, *inexperienced* is what she said, but not like that, you know?"

"Yes," I said, my stomach on the floor. You were dumping me because your sister said so?

"And, OK, I see what she means, but she doesn't, Min, know what she's talking about. She's so, everybody's so

197

stupid, you know? Christian too, Todd, whoever says stupid things, you're from different worlds, like you dropped here in a spaceship."

I had to say something. "Yeah," I said. "So—?"

"So they can *fuck* themselves," you said. "I don't care, you know?"

I felt a smile on my face, tears too.

"Because Min, I *know*, OK? I'm stupid I know, about faggy movies, sorry, fuck, I'm stupid about that too. *No offense*. Ha! But I want to do it, Min. Any party you want, anything, not go to bonfires. Whatever you want to do, for the eighty-ninth birthday, even though I can't remember the name."

"Lottie Carson." I stepped close to you, but you held your hands out, you weren't done.

"And they'll say things, right? I know they will, of course they will. Your friends are, probably, too, right?"

"*Yes*," I said. I felt furious, or furiously *something*, pacing with you and waiting to fall into your moving arms.

"*Yes*," you said, with a huge grin. "Let's stay together, I want to be with you. Let's. Yes?"

"*Yes.*"

"Because I don't care, virginity, different, arty, weird parties with bad cake, that igloo. Just *together*, Min."

"Yes."

"Like everyone is telling us not to be."

"Yes!"

"Because Min, listen, I love you."

I gaped.

"Don't, you don't have to—I know it's crazy, Joan says I've really lost it, but—"

"I love you too," I said.

"You don't have to—"

"I've been wanting to," I said, "say it. But everyone says—"

"Yeah," you said. "Me too. But I do."

"Yes," I said. "I don't care what they say about it, any word of what they say."

"I love you," you said again, and then you stopped and we went at it, laughing and hungry on the sofa with our mouths open in a long, desperate kiss, sliding off to the floor, which was hard, *ouch*, too hard without the cushions there. We were laughing. We kissed more, but it was uncomfortable on the floor.

"What happened to the cushions?"

"Joan did that too," you said. "But fuck that and fuck her."

I laughed.

"What do you want to do now, Min?"

"I want to try the Pensieri."

You blinked. "What?"

"The liquor for the cookies," I said. "I got it. I want to

try it." I hoped you wouldn't ask where I got it, and you didn't, so I never told you.

"The liquor for the cookies," you said. "OK. Yes. Where is it?"

I went and got it, no glasses, just twisted at the top until it was open and the strange rich smell was in my face, like wine but with something running through it, herbal or mineral, dazzling and weird. "You first," I said, and handed it over. You frowned into the bottle, then smiled at me and took a slow swig and immediately spat it out down your T-shirt.

"Criminy!" you shrieked. "That is, what is that? It tastes like somebody killed a spicy fig. What's in that?"

I was laughing too hard to answer. You grinned and threw off your T-shirt. "I don't even want to touch it! Criminy, it's on my pants!" You tried to pour the bottle into my shrieky mouth, spilled it on my top. I squealed and grabbed it, threatening Pensieri everywhere like a hand grenade, you undid your pants smiling, I felt the liquor sticky on my skin and put the bottle down, took off my shirt without unbuttoning it, a ripping sound, a button skittering under the television, heaving there in my bra, laughing at you struggling with the last bit of your jeans. I've seen *Now Calls the Wilderness* on the big screen, Ed, I've seen a fully restored print of *The Acrobats*. I have never seen anything so very beautiful as you in your underwear like a little boy, then naked, hooting with laughter, the drink a streak on your chest, excited,

200

looking at me in the living room. I kept that beautiful sight deep inside me, all the way home hours later, the Pensieri in the pocket of the coat I bought you, which you gave back to me because the weather had gotten cold and worse, wrapping me in what you'd never wear again, buttoning it so it might hide my ruined top, all the way home thinking of your laughing naked face. Nothing else came close. Not even what you managed to do with me later, breathless and open and flushed after I answered your next question, patient with your fingers and your mouth so warm on me I could not tell one from the other, what no boy could ever pull off because no boy asked so sweet and happily for help, as terrific and gasping as it was, not even that overcame the sight of you there laughing. I never told you that, even after telling you I love you, all those times all that day, I never told you how beautiful it was then, like everyone was telling us not to be. I never told you that, it was too tremendous a thing to tell until now in tears in Leopardi's with my friend restored to me, just something to gaze at in the light of that gorgeous morning smiling at me smiling at you.

"And now, Min," you asked me then in a pant, "what do you want to do now?" and I'm flushing now at what I said then.

AND the PERFECT
IS GONE FROM THEM

Indelible is the word the book uses, *When the Lights Go Down*, indelible images is what they keep saying. The brass mask of the emperor, floating faceup in the churning water before slowly sinking into black in *Realm of Rage*. Patricia Ocampo's sad, contemptuous gaze at the departing stage-coach in *The Last Days of El Paso*. Paolo Arnold scream-ing at the sky and carving the Sphinx. Bette Madsen's legs they call indelible, the splits she does in *What a Hoot!* with those impossible stockings, the children playing as the assas-sin bleeds on the other side of the fence is indelible in *The Body Is a Machine (Le corps est une machine)*, the flying saucers in *The Flying Saucers!* indelible too. All it means is, I looked it up online to be sure, stays in your head. I'd only heard it about ink.

One I have is me in the empty band shell of Bluebeard Gardens. I can see it: I was wearing jeans, the green top you told me you like but probably couldn't pick out of a line-up now, my black Chinese slippers falling off my feet, my sweater tied and drooping around my waist because it was sweaty to walk all that way from the bus. Sitting where they play the marches for the Fourth of July, where long-past-cool folk singers come to sing for free about overcoming injustice, just cold gray cement in the off-season, with dead leaves and the occasional squirrel in a frantic hurry. And me, sitting with my legs stretched out in a V, eating the pistachios your sister spiced and put in this elegant tin for you. It'll never fade. It's not what I saw—it's not something I could have possibly seen—because we were together there, but when I see it, you're not in the picture. In the indelible image, I am alone eating the pistachios and lin-ing up perfectly the shells in half circles getting smaller and smaller like parentheses in parentheses. Really, you were just checking for electricity.

"There is," you called happily from behind a pile of tarps, "a whole row of outlets here."

"Working?"

"Should I stick my finger in them? I'm sure they're

working. Who would turn them off? Enough for lights and music. Joan's old boom box thing should do it, it's ugly but loud."

"And lights?"

"We have Christmas lights, but it's a pain to get them. Do you have them somewhere better than our messy attic?"

I waited.

"Oh, right."

"Right."

"No Christmas for you."

"No Christmas for me," I said.

"But Hanukkah lights?" you said, bounding back to me. "They have those. I mean, it's the Festival of Lights, right?"

"How do you know that?"

"I read about Jewish. I wanted to know."

"Come on."

"Annette told me," you admitted, frowning a pistachio open. "But *she* read it someplace."

"Well, I don't have them. I'll help you get them out of the attic. They're not *too* Christmas-y, are they?"

"White, some of them are."

"Perfect," I said, and stretched my legs out further. You stood over me watching, munched, pleased.

"Is it?"

"Yes," I said.

"And you laughed."

"I didn't *laugh*."

"But you didn't think of it," you said, and did a few quick steps back and forth on the stage, athletic and cute. It was perfect, Bluebeard Gardens, fashioned crumbly and quaint like *Stage Door Kisses* or *And Now the Trumpets*. There were chairs down in the audience to sit in. Space for dancing, a platform where we could put the food. And out past the stage and the seats, the beautiful statues would keep stern and silent watch. Soldiers and politicians, composers and Irishmen, all along the perimeter, angry on horseback or proud with a staff. A turtle with the world on its back. A few modern things, a big black triangle, three shapes on top of one another, surely a spooky shadow at night. An Indian chief, nurses of the Civil War, the man who discovered something, the ivy too thick on the plaque to see, a test tube in his hand where birds had shat, a clipboard held at his side. Two women in robes representing the Arts and Nature, given to us from our sister city of somewhere in Norway. If we invited no one, it would still be a beautiful crowd of glamour, the commodore, the ballerina, the dragon for the Year of the Dragon 1916. I'd been here before as a kid for a few picnics, but my dad always said, I can hear him now, indelible, it was too loud. But without the hullabaloo it was the perfect, perfect place for Lottie Carson's eighty-ninth birthday party.

"Are there cops here at night, I wonder," I wondered.

"No."

"How do you know?"

"Amy and I used to hang out here. She lived up on Lapp, just one block there. You can see the lions from her porch."

"Amy?"

"Amy Simon. Sophomore year. She moved, her dad got transferred. Real asshole, that guy, strict and paranoid. So we used to sneak here."

"So I'm not the first girl you've gotten naked in a park?" I said, smiling and thinking about this. I began to drop the shells one by one into this tin.

You looked up at the curve of the band shell for a sec, *perfect if it rains*, you'd told me. You'd thought of everything, you'd been thinking about the party, all by yourself. "You are, actually," you said. "You're the only one. But you're not the only one I *tried* to get naked in a park."

I laughed a little, dropped a few more in. "I guess I can't blame you for trying."

"No other girl," you said. "Nobody else ever did anything but freak out if I mentioned any other girl."

"I'm different, I know," I said, a little bored of that.

"I don't mean *that*," you said. "I mean, I love you."

Every time you said it, you really said it. It wasn't like a sequel where Hollywood just lines up the same actors and hopes it works again. It was like a remake, with a new director and crew trying something else and starting from scratch.

"I love you too."

"I can't believe this is what you want."

"What," I said, "you?"

"No, I mean planning a party. Finding a park, just *showing* it to you, and you act like I did something."

"You *did*. This *is*."

"I mean, with my friends—we buy stupid things for our girlfriends."

"Yeah, I've seen that around."

"Teddy bears, candy things, magazines even. Don't say it's stupid, because we all think so, everybody, but it's what we do. What do you guys do? Poems or something, right? I'm not going to write you a poem."

Joe, actually, used to write me poems. Once, one of them was a sonnet. Those I gave back in an envelope. "I know. This is—I like *this*, Ed. This is a perfect place."

"And I can't buy you flowers, because we haven't had a fight yet, really."

"And I told you never to buy me flowers," and I can see it, you rolling your eyes and smiling on the stage. I smiled back, an idiot who didn't want flowers, the fucking flower shop where everything collapsed, why the bottom of this box is carpeted with dead rose petals like a shrine on the highway where there's been a wreck.

"Do we have to go?"

We were skipping, but I had a test. "We have time, a little."

"Gosh," you said, "what can me and my girlfriend do in a park—"

"Nope," I said. "A, too cold."

You leaned down and gave me a lengthy kiss. "And B?"

"Actually that's the only reason I can think of, is A."

Your hands moved. "It's not *that* cold," you said. "We wouldn't have to take *everything* off."

"Ed—"

"I mean, we wouldn't have to do a lot."

I shrugged out of your arms, put the last shells in. "My test," I said.

"OK, OK."

"But thanks for taking me here. You're right."

"I told you it was perfect."

"So for the party we have food—"

"Drink. Trevor said he'd do it. But it can't just be champagne, it's too word-I'm-not-allowed-to-say."

"OK. And Trevor won't be an asshole at the party?"

"Oh," you said, "I guarantee he will. But not, you know, too much."

"OK, so food, drink, music, lights. Everything but invitations and a guest list."

"Everything but," you said, with a tiny smirk. I threw a shell at you and then stood up to get it. I didn't know why, not then. There was no reason to keep them, unremarkable nothings, even now they look like anything else.

209

But everything else is gone. *I mean, I love you* is gone, and your dance upon the stage, and all the perfection for the party. Even the party would have been gone, had we ever had it, the music back to Joan, the lights back in your attic, the food digested and the drinks thrown up, Lottie Carson driven home very politely and helped through her own sculpture garden to her front door late, late at night, tired from the lovely celebration, thankful and calling us *dear*. All gone, indelible but invisible, not quite everything but *everything but*. Mr. Nelson said it went on my permanent record, fifteen minutes late on a test day, but that's gone too, along with my B- and the essay question I totally bluffed through, and gone is the reason I was late, how I ran to you and kissed your neck and pressed my hand against you, murmuring that it seemed like *everything but* felt pretty good to you. We didn't do a lot, as you promised. We did a little, and the little is gone, those twenty-whatnot minutes scurried away wherever the actors go when the movie's over and we're blinking at the lights of the exit signs, wherever the old loves go when they move away with their asshole dads or just look elsewhere when I walk by in the halls. And the feeling, the real perfect of that afternoon, that you were thinking about me, that you'd remembered this garden and waited outside geometry to get me to skip class and see what you knew I'd love—that feeling's gone forever too.

But these are here, Ed. Look at them, weighty now and heavy-making on the heart when I open the tin and rattle them in my hands sore from writing you. They've been made indelible, Ed, because everything else has vanished, so you take them now. Maybe if you're the one keeping them, I'll be the one feeling better.

METROPOLITAN
MULTIPLEX
CINEMAS
GOOFBALLS III
$10.50
STUDENT
mmc
PG-13
3:30
PLEASE HOLD ON
TO THIS TICKET
ENJOY
THE FILM

There's that scene in *Verdict Written in Tears*, where Karl Braughton as the prosecutor throws down the bouquet of roses, and slowly, slowly the camera moves down the blossoms and the stems, past the leaves and thorns, to the ribbon that holds them together—pale blue they say, but it's a black-and-white movie—down the lawyer's book-piled table to the parquet floor, slowly, slowly crawling its way to the witness box. And all the while we hear Amelia Hardwick sputtering with indignation, accusation, justification, hysteria, and finally when the lens reaches her, the shame, the deep, horrifying shame of realizing it must be true. She *is* a murderess. She *was* in the gazebo that quiet afternoon. Her amnesia is *real*, not part of a frame-up by her mother-in-law. And she cries the helpless cry of the end of the movie, the evidence inescapable, like a curtain closing.

I have amnesia about *Goofballs III*. If Karl Braughton, with his thumbs in his suspenders, said to me, "Min Green, do you *swear* you have not seen a single frame of the *Goofballs* franchise?" I would look first at the solemn jurors and then at Sidney Juno—who's not in the movie but so gorgeous I'd slip him in there—and I would say yes, *yes*, I would say, because those movies are so fucking stupid my teeth ache to gnash them apart. But here are the tickets thrown in my face from this closet box of grief. So watch me grovel denying it.

Al just saw and said "*Goofballs III*?!" in disbelief to me. I'd slap him, but it's still delicate between us.

You wanted to go, Ed, I will tell him, so go we went. I kept looking around the sparse theater until you asked me if I wanted a burka so none of my word-you're-not-allowed-to-say friends would see me here seeing my first *Goofballs* movie. (I bet you say it all the time now, don't you, Ed? Gay gay *gay*.) Really, I wasn't looking for friends, I just wanted to see if there was another female in the audience. And there was. She was chaperoning a birthday party of eleven-year-olds. This I remember, but the movie's lost to amnesia because, Ed, of what you said to me just as the lights went down and they started that catastrophic parade of

214

commercials for automobiles and community colleges and whatnot that the Carnelian would never in a million years play before a movie but that the Metro does without thinking, though from a purely aesthetic point of view, I must admit the one for Burly Soda is pretty cool. You turned to me and said, the combat-ready vehicle flickering on your face, "Remind me when we eat that there's something I want to talk to you about."

"What?"

"Remind me when we eat—"

"No, what is it?"

"Well, there's something unavoidable coming up next weekend, and I think we should figure out how to do it."

It was like a giant spatula had descended hard and splattery onto me. I sat flattened, a sudden and stunned patty, piece of meat in the boy-filled theater. *Unavoidable?* Us having sex? Our fucking *fucking*, unavoidable? Like I couldn't avoid it, the next weekend? You put your arm around me. I made sure my legs were together, even with my knee, the closest one to you, jumpy and jumping. *How to do it?* I was stuttery furious but too something else—meek, in love with you, *something*—to say something. *Goofballs III* descended and I saw none of it. Not one frame, gentlemen of the jury, not a single shot. If I pouted you'd think it was because of the movie, so I held still, tried to pause my brain, think of nothing, etc. I tried not to have a feeling, that I'd not known you'd get like this sometime eventually, what with being Ed Slaterton and everything, entitled to the *unavoidable* intercourse. But the movie, the horny movie of finger-clenching jokes, it is erased and forgotten. And what gets me now, Al staring at these tickets like he found my KKK membership card, is that I'm not the amnesiac I used to be. It's you, I bet, who has forgotten this, Metro three-thirty show, you paid, I think. And Ed, everything else.

"You thought *what?*" you said. We were at Lopsided's, a return to the scene of the sugar heist, eating whatever the meal is that boys eat in the afternoon that's not lunch or dinner or large popcorn at the movies, today a club sandwich and fries, for me tea, reminding myself for the foreverteenth time to put good tea in my purse for when we go to diners. "You thought, actually, that right before the movie started that I was like, next weekend you're losing your," hushed down and leaned forward so it would be none of Lopsided's's business, "virginity? Like, by the way, darling? What kind of cuckoo do you think I am?"

"The kind that says *cuckoo*."

"And this is how you sat through that movie. That's why? No wonder you didn't like it."

I let my relief breathe all around me, like I'd jumped into a perfect pool and was waiting that lovely still moment before starting to swim. "Yep. That's why I didn't like *Goofballs III: Look Out Below!*"

"Well, I'd be willing to see it again."

"Shut up."

"I *would*! For you, so you could concentrate."

"That's awful sweet. No thanks."

"Maybe you should check in that precious film book of yours to see if it's cool to like it first."

"Maybe you should check with that precious coach of yours to see if it's good for your game."

"Coach loves those movies. He took the whole team to *Goofballs II* at the end of last season."

I looked at you, all I had. Al hadn't even called me, even after I called and hung up when he answered. I couldn't go over this with him and never will. "The sad thing is that I have no idea if you're kidding."

"Yeah, you definitely can't tell what I'm saying today. *Unavoidable*, criminy. I told you before we're not on a schedule, there's no prize."

"OK, then what did you mean? What's next weekend?"

"Halloween, you dope."

"What?"

"Well, you're going to want to do the thing your crowd does that's all arty and word-I'm-not-allowed-to-say."

"It's just a party."

"So's mine."

"Yeah, on the football field, with three kids getting expelled every year."

You nodded, smiled, sighed, looking sad at your finished plate like you wanted to eat a club sandwich and fries all over again. "I still miss Andy."

I sighed too, and you poked your fancy, flaggy toothpick right on the boundary between us. Who knows why the Earth evolved the way it did, but after years of shameful Halloween drunken debauchery at high school gatherings every year, the Civic Whatever Association decided to take a stance against shameful Halloween drunken debauchery at high school gatherings by combining all of the high school gatherings into one morass of shameful Halloween drunken debauchery on a football field, this year Hellman's football field, called the All-City Halloween Bash, with all the teams from all the schools, except swimming, coordinated in costumes and competing for stupid gift-certificate prizes in a contest on the risers that always degenerates into girls taking off their tops, the parking lot a whole carpeted ocean of vomit from the kegs lined up in trunks apparently invisible to the chaperoning coaches always dressed in the same pudgy Superman outfits with fake foam muscles looking lumpy and cancerous in the floodlights. Or so I've seen in the yearbook photos, because I'd never gone, because my allegiance is under the other flag, the other morass of shameful Halloween drunken debauchery, the one where all the drama and arts clubs from all the high schools pool the money they make selling candy every year at intermission in auditoriums and all-purpose rooms across the city at their productions of *Don't Tell Mummy!* and *Summer Clouds* and *My Town, Your Town* and *Gadzooks!* to rent a space and force all the stupid student councils at all the stupid schools to rotate turns sitting in a room and on e-mail arguing over a theme and decorations and postering everywhere and let's not even think about the costumes, elaborate with real machinery and feathers and dialogue performed on a make-shift stage to win stupid gift-certificate prizes in a contest that always degenerates into a lascivious pit of improvised dance when like always the Shrouded Skulls take the stage as they will until the sun implodes in a swirl of dry ice and mirror ball and start playing "Snarl at Me, Sweetheart," the singer eyelining around the room looking for the ingenue costumed in angel wings he'll take out to his hearse in a cloud of clove cigarettes when his set's over. I was tired of it, I never liked it, but of course I was going, just like you were going to the All-City Halloween Bash, the Ball and the Bash, and everybody chooses sides.

"Where is it this year?" you asked me.

"The Scandinavian Hall."

"What's the theme?"

"Pure Evil. Do you guys, does it even have a theme?"

"No." We grinned grimly at each other, you thinking that it was worse to have a theme and me thinking that it was worse not to have one but at least both thinking that it was basically lame no matter what.

"Will your friends freak," you asked, "if you don't—"

"I *have* to go," I said. "My friends hate me already, I have to go. But you won't be noticed if you're not there, right?"

"Min, the team already has their costumes."

"I was kidding," I said, unhappily and lying. "What are you guys?"

"Chain gang."

"Isn't that racist?"

"I think they let anyone into a chain gang, Min. What are you?"

"I don't know, I always last-minute it. Last year I was yellow journalism, not my best. People thought I was the newspapers the dog pees on."

You laughed into your ice water and took two things out of your back pocket, one something very cute for you, the other a pen. "Let's make a plan."

"We could call in sick to our friends. The Carnelian always has a Kramer Horror Marathon on Halloween."

"Nobody will fall for that. No, I mean a *plan*." You pinched three napkins out of the holder and laid one flat. A new frontier. Biting your lip like you do, you sketched out a few things, unwavering and neat, though I was the one who moved your plate away so you would have room to see it through. I smiled and smiled at you and kept forgetting to look at the napkin until you caught me and tapped with your pen.

"OK, this is school."

"You're very cute when you do this."

"Min."

"You *are*. Do you do this all the time?"

"You've seen me do this. Like my sketches for the party."

"You made sketches for the *party*?"

"Oops, wasn't you. I was trying to figure how the lights would get strung up. It was, um, oh yeah, in government, with Annette it must have been. But yes, I do it, it helps me think. You know how I am with the math and stuff."

"You know I love you," I said. "OK, this is school. Wait, where's the gym?"

"Doesn't matter, not in the plan."

"OK. So the yard is *here*."

"It's a football field. Don't call it a yard."

"Grass where people sit and hang out is a yard."

"We stole things here, but that doesn't make it a bank."

You were getting better at talking like this with me,

the bounce-bounce dialogue that's so good in all the *Old Hat* movies. I ruffled your hair. "OK, there's your precious football field. Now draw a gazillion drunks in costume."

"We'll see them soon enough. Now way up here's the Scandinavian thing, somewhere around here."

"It's right at the edge of that cemetery, so that's—"

"OK, here," you said, scritching the park in a neat shape, and then the whole neighborhood between. Perfect.

"Do you always use that?"

"This? Yes. Let's not start saying the other one is a nerd, because I will win that game."

"I'm not. I like it."

You rolled your eyes and didn't believe me, but it was true, Ed, I loved the way your mathy brain powered you on across the napkin. "*There*," you said, finishing a line. "Now, too far to walk, right?"

"From where?"

"Between them. I mean, we have to go to both, right?"

I leaned over our high school and kissed you.

"But we can't walk," you said, thinking so hard the kiss just got a brief smile. "So, bus. But the bus goes this way, down here someplace and then around." You must have looked the same way when you were a kid, I thought, thinking I should ask Joan to see old pictures. You just trailed off where the bus went when we didn't care, half this map in strict order and the other half just loose ink, like

225

how I knew you and how I thought I knew you. "That doesn't look good either. The bus won't work."

"What about that other line, the something route, over here?"

"Oh yeah. The 6 it is, I think. Like here, and then *here*."

We looked at it. "Will your sister," I said—

"No way. She never lets me drive any night when anyone might be drinking. And let's face it."

"Yeah," I said. The lines were straighter than anyone would be going that night. "Hey, the 6 ends up here, this end of Dexter, right?"

"Oh yeah. I remember from going out with Marjorie."

"She lives out here?"

"No, she took ballet at the weird place around here."

"So," I said, taking your pen and dotting it out, "we start at your Bash, sneak out this way, probably where people will think we're just going to fool around."

"Which we will," you said, taking it back, marking an X which I blushed at and ignored.

"And then we take the bus here and get off *here* and refortify at In the Cups. I can't draw a cup. Then walk whatever it is, eight blocks, *dot dot dot*, and catch the 6 and stop here. And then we walk across and we're at the Ball. *Voilà!*"

You blinked at me, didn't *voilà!* back. My dotted lines all over your neatness. "Across the cemetery at night?"

"You'll be safe," I said. "You'll be with the co-captain of the basketball team, oh wait, that's me."

"Not safety," you said. "Oh, forget it," and I remembered what's famous about the cemetery, or *famous* isn't the word, but why nobody hangs out there. Every place has them, I guess, a park or place where men go at night to do it to each other secret in the dark.

"We'll keep our eyes closed," I said, "so the gay won't be catching."

"If I can't say *gay* you can't."

"You can say *gay*," I said, "when you're actually talking about gay. And how do you even know about the cemetery thing?"

"Tell me first how *you* know."

"I drop Al off there most nights," I said, the joke sticking in my throat.

You covered your face, *my girlfriend is so nuts.* "Well, yeah," you tried bravely, "I see him there when I pit-stop to relieve the tension of *everything but.*"

"Shut up," I said. "You love *everything but.*"

"I do," you grinned. "Um, but speaking of. I wanted to—"

"Yeah?"

"My sister—"

"Ew. Speaking of *that*, your sister?"

"Stop it. She's going away."

"What?"

227

"For the weekend. Not next, not Halloween, but after that."

"And?"

"And my mom's not back," you said, "so I'll have the house. You could, you know—"

"Yeah, I know."

"*Sleep over* is all I was going to say, Min."

"You also said there wasn't a schedule. *Just* said it."

"There wasn't. *Isn't*. But I just—"

"I don't want to lose my virginity in your bed," I said.

You sighed at the napkin. "Do you mean that, like, not in my bed or not with me?"

"Just the actual bed," I said. "Or your car or a *park*. Somewhere, you'll laugh, somewhere extraordinary."

You did, I'll give you that Ed, not laugh. "Extraordinary."

"Extraordinary," I said.

"OK," you said, and then smiled. "Tommy and Amber lost it in her dad's warehouse."

"Ed."

"They did! Between two refrigerators!"

"Not that kind of—"

"I know, I know. Don't worry, Min. It's not the cuckoo thing you thought I said, *unavoidable*. I want you to be, I can't find the word I mean." You sighed again. "*Happy*. Which is why we're going to take two buses and walk through a gay place Halloween night."

228

I couldn't decide about that *gay*, let it slide. "We'll have fun," I lied.

"Maybe the following weekend we will," you said shyly, and right then I wanted to, an eager hunger in my mouth and my lap. I had such a feeling. Fill it with something else instead, I thought, but what I didn't know.

"Maybe," I said finally.

"This is complicated," you said, back on the napkin, and then looked at me. You wanted to pry me open, I could see it, drag me across our boundaries so we could feast together in secret from the rest of the world. "But," you said, "no, not *but*. I love you."

Coffee, I thought, was what. "Let's drink to it," I said.

"Life-giving brew," you agreed, all energy and spiky delight. You waved for the waitress, started to crumple our plan.

"Wait, wait."

"What?"

"I want that. Don't shred our plan."

"We'll remember it without it."

"I still want it."

"You're not," you said, "going to tell Al or somebody that I make these I-won't-say-it charts."

"I will not," I said in a sad promise, "tell Al. It's just for me."

"Just for you?" you said. "OK." You hunched over for

a sec while I ordered the coffee, ignoring the looks of the waitress looking at you. You handed it to me, but I'd already grabbed what I wanted, thefted again at Lopsided's, distracted you with chatter until the coffee came and you forgot it was gone. But you put one over on me, too, the other side of the napkin I discovered too late, not when I got home, not when I dropped it into the box, only heartbroken and weepy when it wasn't true anymore. Just like we discovered as the waitress plunked down coffee and the bill and stalked off that there wasn't any sugar at our table: when it was too late, Ed, to do any good.

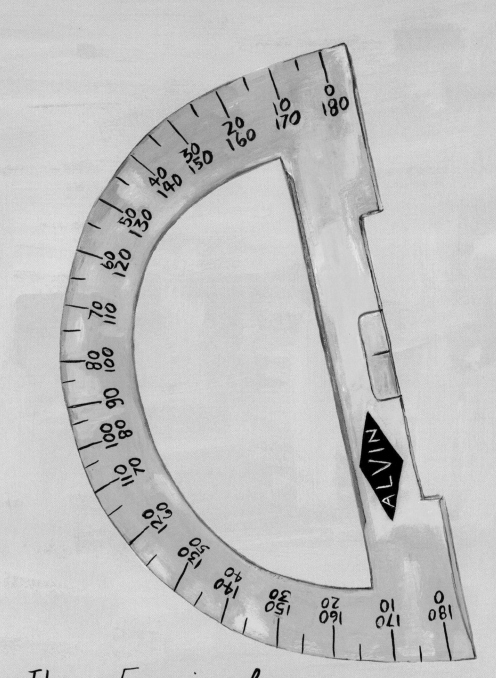

I'm a FOOL is whAT

This is what I stole. Here's it back. I thought, my goddamn ex-love, that it was cute that you carried this around to help you map out your thinking. Cute in your pocket all the time. I'm not a cuckoo, either. I'm a fool is what.

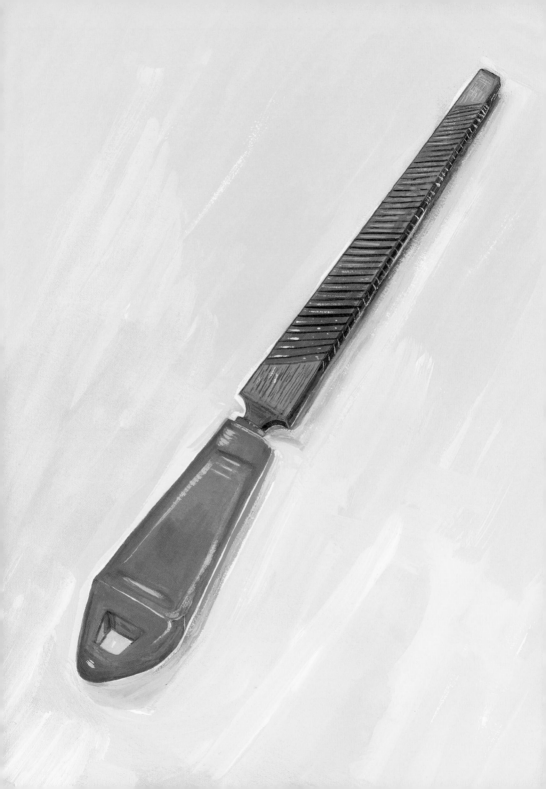

And you never saw this, either. I stood alone with it in my hands in Green Mountain Hardware, quiet and lonely and trying to conjure Al beside me so I could ask him things only he could know. Is this really a file, like a file they use in *We Break at Dawn* or *Fugitives by Moonlight* to run free with the dogs after them and the barbed wire silhouetted against the floodlights? Al and I had seen that double feature as part of the Carnelian's Prison Week, which hilariously conclud-ed with the Meyers documentary on boarding schools. The theater was almost empty that day, who in the world else could I ask? The Green Mountain staff in their vests and headsets cannot be asked, *Is this metal file oven-safe?* Picturing us, you and me, in an accidental iron-poisoning suicide pact from the surprise I wanted us to share. I wanted so badly to call Al and say "I know we're mad at each other forever maybe, but could you just tell me this one single thing about metal and cooking?" but of course not. *Joan*, I thought, I could ask Joan maybe, and then she came around the corner.

"Hey, Min."

"Annette, hi."

"What are you doing here?"

"Halloween shopping," I said, holding up the file.

"Wow, me too," she said. "I need chains. Come with?"

We walked toward where they were, a row of shiny wheels you could unwind and buy by the yard. Annette eyed through them like it was real jewelry, stopping to lay her whole bare arm against them. "What are you going to be?" I asked her.

"I'm trying to see how they feel," she said. "I don't know, it's kind of a medieval thing I'm doing with someone. You know, but *slinky*."

Slutty, is what I thought. All the girls who date athletes are slutty in their costumes, slutty witch, slutty cat, slutty hooker.

"Can I wear these with no bra, do you think?"

"Really?" I tried not to squeal.

"I mean, wrapped around like a tube top kind of. I'm not that big."

"I think you'll be bruised by the end of the night," I said.

She turned to glare. "Are you threatening me?" she said.

"What? *No!*"

"Kidding, Min. *Kidding*. Ed told me *he's* the one who doesn't get *your* jokes. Criminy, as he would say."

"Criminy," I agreed dumbly.

"What's that thing for?"

"I haven't decided really," I said. "I was thinking, you know how Ed's a prisoner?"

"The chain gang, yeah."

"Well, you know how in old prison movies they bake a file in a cake? You know, to saw away the bars or something. Like a loyal wife helping, keeping the car running outside the back entrance."

She looked dubiously at the file. "You're Ed's *wife* for Halloween?"

She was smiling, but it was like she'd dumped a sack of stupid on my head. I felt slovenly with her glittered eyes on me, moronic in fat pants and shoes. "No," I said. "I was just going to make him a cake to get him in the mood that day."

"As I remember, he's always in the mood," Annette said, with a little smile.

"You know what I mean."

"I do. So what are you going to be really?"

"The warden," I said.

"What?"

"Like, in charge of the prison?"

"Oh yeah. Cool."

"It's lame I know, but I have this coat of my dad's to wear."

"Cool," she said again, unraveling her choice.

"I couldn't, you know. I'm not the type for, like, the sexy costume."

She paused and really looked me over, probably for the first time I thought. "You totally are, Min. It's just—" and she bit her lip like *never mind*.

"What?"

"Well, you're, I know you're going to hate this."

"What?"

"Um—"

"You're going to say *arty.*"

"I'm saying what Ed is always saying. You're different, you don't need to do this kind of thing." She held up the chain scornfully. "You have a body, you do, you're beautiful and everything. But then you have everything else too. That's why everyone's jealous of you, Min."

"They're not jealous."

"Yes," she said almost angrily to the chains. "They are."

"Well, if they're jealous, it's just because I'm with Ed Slaterton, it's not because of me," I said.

"That is why," she said, and shook her hair. "But it's you who got him." She nodded at my file. "You'd better carry a weapon Saturday night. All the girls will be vampire Cleopatras trying to claw him away from you."

She laughed and I decided to laugh too. *Kidding*, I said to myself, and then out loud, "Catfight. The boys will love that, girl on girl."

"We could charge admission," she said, pretending to claw at me. "You ready to go?"

I'd decided, absolutely, not to buy this stupid file. I followed her to the cash register with it in my hands while she bubbled her way with the cashier, who snipped the chain and gave her a discount. Mine gave me my change and a receipt.

"You want to go get a juice or something dumb like that?"

"No, thanks," I said, following her out. "I gotta go home and do the rest of the costume."

"You didn't freak out about what I said about Saturday, did you? It was a joke."

"No," I said.

"Well, sort of a joke," she said with a smile, switching hands with the bag of chains. "I mean, everybody knows he's yours."

"Not Jillian."

"Jillian's a *bitch*," she said, too fiercely.

"Whoa."

"Long story, Min. But don't worry about her."

I looked sadly out at the wet traffic. It had been raining, my Jewish hair a hideous cloud of pollution, and it was going to rain some more. I felt unshielded there outside Green Mountain, sensitive as a match flame, a lost baby something in the streets, without a mother or a collar or a cardboard box to call home. "I worry about everyone," I said, why not let out the honest answer. "*Different*, everyone keeps saying different. He's mine now but you're right, someone could take him. I'm like an outsider to everyone else he knows."

She didn't bother saying I was wrong. "No," she said. "He loves you."

"And I love him," I said, though what I wanted to say was *thank you*. I thought, the idiot that I was, the fool with a file in a bag, that she was looking out for me.

"*And love, who can say the way it winds,*" she recited, "*like a serpent in the garden of our untroubled minds.*"

"What's that?"

"Salleford," she said. "Alice Salleford. Sophomore English. And I thought you were the arty one."

"I'm not arty," I said.

"Well, you're something," she said, and gave me a quick hug good-bye, rattly with chains. Sure enough it started to rain. She dashed from awning to awning and gave me a wave before disappearing. Beautiful she was, beautiful in the rain and her clothing. The file clanked against me, my stupid idea nobody would have gotten had I ever done it. You even wouldn't have gotten it, Ed, I thought, watching her go. It's why we broke up, so here it is. Ed, how could you?

This isn't yours. It was left in an envelope taped to my locker, my name not even written on it. I thought it was something from you, but it just dropped into my hand, no note. I felt Al's anger, sulky, honorable, goddamn furious in my hands as I held this. My free ticket, earned by helping him tape up posters. Goddamn subcommittee. He could have made me buy one, but instead there it was, a ticked-off gift. It's not yours, but I'm giving it back to you because it's your fault. The drama clubbers have these fancy tokens made instead of tickets so you can wear them around your neck all year if you're extra goth embarrassing to prove you went to the All-City All Hallows' Ball. I never keep mine, just shove them in a drawer or whatever. HOPE, what a laugh. It's a reminder of the night, let's admit it now together—Halloween of Pure Evil—the night we should have broken up.

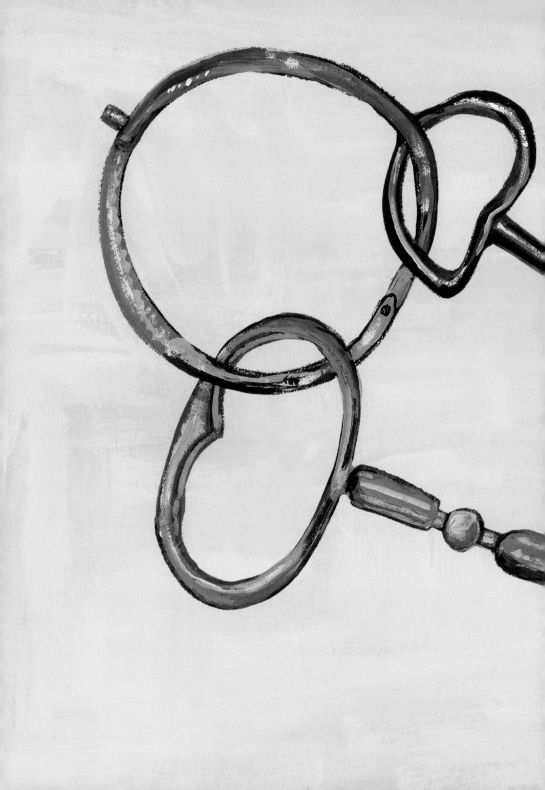

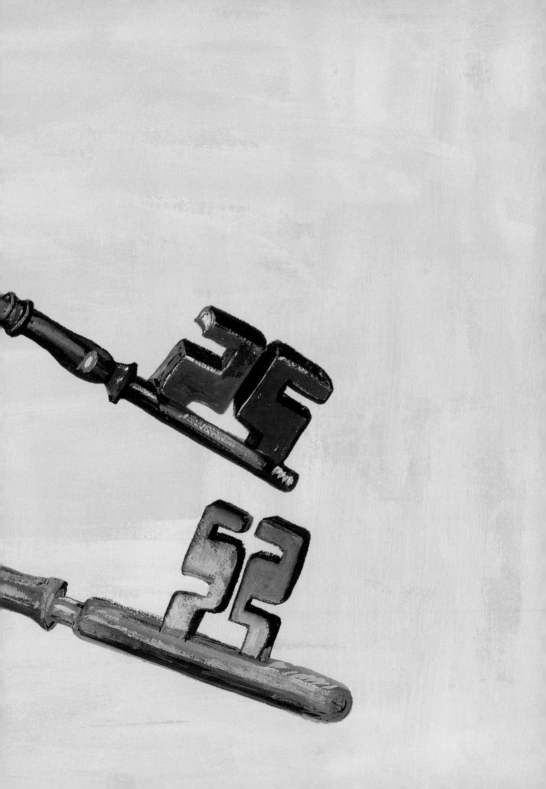

So why *did* we break up? When I think of it now, think of it really, I think of how tired I was Halloween Saturday, from getting up early to sneak off to Tip Top Goods myself to buy these, which I never gave you. Yawning outside later, spray-painting an old thrift-store cap I used to wear freshman year, squinting at the gray to see if it matched my dad's coat, Hawk Davies floating out my bedroom window to bask all over me, that cool part of "Take Another Train" when he polishes off a solo and you hear someone's faint cry of appreciation, *Yeah Hawk yeah* while I grinned in the clear air. It wasn't going to rain out. You and I were going to the Bash and the Ball and it would be OK—extraordinary, even. I had no feeling of otherwise. I can see my happiness, I can see it and I can say that we were happy too then, not just me. I guess I can cling to anything.

"It's good to see you happy," my mom said, coming out with steaming tea. I'd been coiled up thinking she was telling me the jazz was too loud, think of the neighbors.

"Thanks," I said for the Earl Grey.

"Even if it is in your father's coat," she said, this year's thing of deciding it was OK to talk crap about Dad.

"Just for you, Mom, I'll try to ruin it tonight."

She laughed a little. "How?"

"Um, I'll spill drugs on it and roll around in the mud."

"When am I going to meet this boy?"

"Mom."

"I just want to meet him."

"You want to approve him."

"I love you," she tried like always. "You're my only daughter, Min."

"What do you want to know?" I said. "He's tall, he's skinny, he's polite. Isn't he polite on the phone?"

"Sure."

"And he's captain of the basketball team."

"Co-captain."

"That means there's another captain too."

"I know what it means, Min. It's just—what do you have in common?"

I took a sip of tea instead of clawing her eyes out. "Thematic Halloween costumes," I said.

"Yes, you told me. The whole team is prisoners and you're playing along."

"It's not *playing along*."

"I know he's popular, Min. Jordan's mother tells me this. I just don't want you led around, like, like somebody's goat."

Goat? "I'm the one being the *warden*," I said. "I'm going to lead *them* around." Not true, of course, but fuck her.

"OK, OK," my mom said. "Well, the costume's coming along. And what are those?"

"Keys," I said. "You know, a warden has keys." For some moron reason I thought I'd include her for a sec. "I thought I'd wear them on my belt, you know? And then at the end of the night I'd give them to Ed."

My mom's eyes widened.

"What?"

"You're going to give Ed those keys?"

"What? It's *my* money."

"But Min, honey," she said, and put her hand on me. My wrists trembled to spray-paint her in the face and make her gray, although, I noticed suddenly but without surprise, she already was. "Isn't that a little, you know?"

"What?"

"Symbolic?"

"What?"

"I mean——"

"*Ew.* Like, a dirty joke? Key in the keyhole?"

"Well, people will think——"

"Nobody thinks like that. Mom, you're *disgusting. Seriously.*"

"Min," she said quietly, her eyes searchlighting all over me. "Are you sleeping with this boy?"

This boy. Goat. You're my daughter. It was like bad food I was force-fed and couldn't keep down. Her fingers were still on me, skittering on my shoulder like a little pair of school scissors, blunt, ineffective, useless, and not the real thing. "It is none," I said, "none, *none* of your business!"

"You're my daughter," she said. "I love you."

I walked three steps down the driveway to look at her, hands on her hips. On newspapers on the ground the hat I was going to wear. Do you know, Ed, how much it fucking punches me in the stomach that my own *mother* was proved right? I must have shouted something and she must have shouted something back and stomped, she must have, into the house. But all I remember is the music fading, vengefully turned down so it no longer sound-tracked the day. Fuck her, I thought. *Yeah Hawk yeah.* I was done anyway.

Though I didn't, did I, give you the keys. The day cooled to dusk while I did a little homework, dozed, missed Al, thought about calling Al, didn't call Al, got dressed, and headed out with a dagger-glare at my mother pouring little candy bars into a bowl she'd sit and eat while waiting for youngsters. The boy I used to babysit was out on the corner throwing eggs at cars while the sun set. He flipped me off. The world was getting worse I guess, like this Japanese remake of *Rip Van Winkle* called *The Gates of Sleep* that Al and I left early from, each time the hero awoke it was more depressing, wife dead, sons drunks, city more polluted, emperors more corrupt, the war dragging on and more and more bloody. Al said that one should have been called *Are You in a Good Mood? We'll Fix That: The Movie.*

I should have known when an old guy on the bus, totally not kidding, thanked me for my service, that my costume was going to be another disaster, but not until I walked under the archway of orange and black balloons looking for you did it really hit me clear, from Jillian Beach of all people. "Oh my God," she said, already tipsy in red-and-white-striped shorts and a bra of blue bandanas. She was porcupined with goose bumps from the evening cool, Annette was right, I didn't have to be afraid of her.

"What?"

"You really are *out there*, Min. A Jewish girl dressing as Hitler?"

"I'm not Hitler."

"They're going to expel you. You're gonna get expelled."

"I'm a warden, Jillian. What are you?"

"Barbara Ross."

"Who?"

"She invented the flag."

"*Betsy*, Jillian. I'll see ya, OK?"

"Ed's not here," she said back to me.

"That's OK," I said, but I didn't even try to be convincing, a Nazi too early for an outdoor party. A nest of freshmen walked around me chattering in mouse ears. A bunch of Draculas preened in a corner. They were already playing that song I hate. The coaches were sipping coffee and sweating in their capes. It was Trevor, who would ever think, who rescued me, limping over with his foot in a cast.

"Hey, Min. Or should I say Officer Green?"

Better a cop than Hitler. "Hey, Trevor. What are you?"

"A guy who broke his foot yesterday and so can't be in the chain gang."

"You'll do anything to get out of dancing onstage."

He laughed loud and pulled a beer out of somewhere. "You *are* funny," he said, as if someone had said otherwise, and took a swig before handing it to me. I could tell he did this with any girl, any person, and that never until me had it been handed back unsipped.

"I'm good."

"Oh yeah," he said. "You don't like beer."

"Ed told you."

"Yeah, why, am I not supposed to know?"

"No, it's fine," I said, looking for you.

"Because, you know, he's always going to tell me."

"Yeah?" I said, and then gave up and looked him in the eye. He was drunk too, as usual, or maybe he was never drunk, I realized I didn't know him well enough to know the difference.

"Yeah," he said. "Slaterton girlfriends need to learn that and scoot if they can't handle it."

"Scoot?"

"Scoot," he said with a wobbly nod. Even drunk, if he was drunk, he was tough-enough-looking to say words like *scoot*. "We talk, Ed and me."

"So what does he say?"

"That he loves you," Trevor said instantly, without embarrassment. "That you passed the test with his sister. That you put up with his math thing. That you're planning a weird movie-star party and that I have to get the fucking *champagne* or he'll kick my ass. And you don't let him say *gay* anymore, which is—can *I* say *gay*?"

"Sure," I said. "*You're* not my boyfriend."

"Thank God," he said, and then, that's where you got it I guess, "no offense."

"None taken," I said.

"I just mean, I don't think we'd get along like that."

"Don't worry about it," I said.

"We're just, I mean, *I* like a fun girl who doesn't change me around with movies or stores that open first thing in the goddamn morning, you know?"

"Yes," I said. "And I wouldn't take you there."

"I'm just, you know, trying to stay fun. Happy on the weekends, you know, sweating hard at practice."

"I get it."

He threw an arm around me like a companionable uncle. "I like you, I don't care what anybody says," he said.

"Thanks," I said, stiff. "I like you too, Trevor."

"Naw," he said, "but you're a good sport about it. I hope you hang around a long time, really I do, and if you don't I hope it's not all drama and shit."

"Um, thanks."

"Now don't get all puckered," he said, finishing a beer and starting another. "I just mean, you guys are like those two planets that crash together in a movie I saw on TV when I was a kid once, the blue people and these weird red guys."

"*When Planets Collide*," I said. "It's a Frank Cranio film. At the end they're all purple."

"*Yeah!*" he said loud, his eyes toggly with wonder and joy. "Nobody I ever knew ever knew that."

"The Carnelian's showing some Cranio in December," I said. "We could double-date, you know, with Ed and whoever girl you're—"

"Not in a million years," he said agreeably. "That theater's *gay.*"

"You say that," I said, "when you're part of a group of guys chained together dancing."

"Not me!" he said, raising his broken foot, and we laughed hard, loud, wild, and I even leaned into him, just as you arrived with your chain gang, everyone in striped pajamas and black plastic loops around their ankles. Underneath your flimsy hat your face was flushed and suspicious. "What the hell, Trev," you said, too loudly, and pulled me away.

"Whoa, whoa," Trevor said, shielding his beer. "We're just goofing, Ed. She's waiting for you."

"And what are you doing, asshole?" you asked him. "Keeping her warm for me?"

"Hey, Ed, happy Halloween, good to see you," I said pointedly like a person. I'd never seen this version, this shouting boy jerk, with your eyes frazzled wrong and your hand a claw on my shoulder. It was nothing I'd seen, but I hadn't, I was thinking, known you that long.

"Dude," Trevor said to you, smirking like the punch line was coming. "Don't accuse like that. You know *everything but*'s not good enough for me."

The whole chain gang oohed. The tears came to me so quick it was like I'd been saving them up for just this thing. I wished I *were* Hitler, I would have killed the whole set of them. "Min!" you called to me, your anger chased away in panic, and even took a few steps toward me. But your gang was chained to you, and they wouldn't let you follow me and make it right. Not that you could. Though you did.

"He's sorry!" one of the stupid boys called, and laughed. "We all did Viper shots to practice our dance, it always makes Slaterton an asshole."

"No way!" Trevor said in jealous delight. "You're doing *Viper*? Where is it where is it where is it?"

You looked helpless at me, and then the party surged around us like the panic in *Last Train Leaving*, the coaches starting off the festivities with their fat, dumpy dance to "I'm the Biggest Man." Go to hell, I thought to everybody, and we were there, everyplace a nightmare of terrible people, screaming, flashing lights, more screaming, worse than a bonfire because there was nothing gorgeous to look at, just the gleamy makeup on people's faces, the rubber masks like roadkill on boys' heads, the slutty costume skin on the girls shiny with sweat, the *thum-thum* thunder from whoever carried in drums, screaming whistles around people's necks like neon nooses, and then the rhythmic chantings, spread out across the crowd as

257

each school started in, different words cropping up for each team, *Eagles! Beavers! Tigers! Marauders!*, a clashing of syllables like the mascots were fighting to the death in the sky, and then the captains hoisted up onto drunken shoulders, each school shouting its competing hero, *McGinn! Thomas! Flinty!* and winning out, *Slaterton! Slaterton! Slaterton!* as the chain gang clumped up to the stage and began their fake-sissy moves to "Love Locked Up" by Andronika, who sounded in the speakers like she also hated this shit, the hoots of the crowd, realizing you were famous even at other schools, your whole linked gang reaching down your pants to your crotches in gross unison and pulling out bottles of Parker's when the lyrics said "Drink every drop," and even with the coaches pretending disapproval the place devastated itself with screaming volume, toppling the cardboard Applause-O-Meter that Natalie Duffin and Jillian were game show gyrating around, and you *won*, triumphant in gift certificates, blowing kisses, bowing awkwardly with your legs tangled up, and then Annette crashing the stage in chains and silver boots and a big stagy ax, kissing the whole gang, *mwah mwah mwah,* just a little longer on you, before raising her weapon and chopping through the chains and setting you free to leap thrilled and drunk, deep into the roaring crowd and vanish for thirty-eight minutes before finding me finally, handsome, beaming, gorgeous, sexy, a winner through and through forever.

I hated you so much.

My face must have blazed with it like Amanda Truewell in *Dance to Forget* when Oliver Shepard walks into the nightclub with his unexpected innocent wife. Fuming and furious hurt, I was bustled away by the surging crowd and was soon trapped at the goalpost with a guy I half knew from homeroom telling me a story about his dad's new wife's white wine problem. I was so angry I knew it would boomerang someplace sometime soon. It growled in me something awful as I just stood frozen and lost. The Bash kept at it, boiling and twisting in costume, until you finally reappeared during the even-worse song, the crowd crying *Hey! Hey! Get down I say!* frantic with your stripes half-unbuttoned and sweaty hair. "I want to tell you something," you said, before I could decide which scathing line I'd been polishing to use first. You held both hands in front of you, spread out, a filthy streak on one palm, like I was about to roll a boulder on you. I stepped back and you stayed there, you stood your ground in the blaring battlefield, and you began to count on your fingers, counting the number of times you were saying what you were saying, both hands twice and then almost again. It was the only thing you could say, the perfect thing, is what you said.

I'm sorry.

I'm sorry.

I'm sorry.

I'm sorry.

I'm sorry.

I'm sorry.

I'm sorry.

I'm sorry.

I'm sorry.

I'm sorry.

I'm sorry.

I'm sorry.

I'm sorry.

I'm sorry.

I'm sorry.

I'm sorry.

I'm sorry.

I'm sorry.

I'm sorry.

I'm sorry.

I'm sorry.

I'm sorry.

I'm sorry.

I'm sorry.

I'm sorry.

"Twenty-six," you said, before I could ask you. Every-one was gathered around, or anyway they were around us, swirling like loud, bad surf. The crowd was low in the mix, a few yelps, a few catcalls. "Twenty-six," you said again, to the crowd, and took a step toward me.

"Don't," I said, though I couldn't decide.

"Twenty-six," you said. "One for each day we've been together, Min." Somebody oohed. Somebody shushed them.

"And I hope that someday I'll do another something stupid and I'll have to say it a million times because that's how long it'll be, together with you, Min. With *you*."

I allowed you another step. The homeroom guy realized he was still there gaping, and stopped and vanished. There was a tremble in my shoulder, behind my knee. I shook my head, shoveling my anger into a shallow grave waiting to be dug up in some plot twist. But, also, your beautiful self, the way you could move and talk to me. I could not look away.

"*Anything*," you said, a vast answer to nothing I'd said. "*Anything*, Min. Anything, anything. If Willows was open, the flowers would be gone, I'd buy every scrap."

"I'm *mad* at you," I said finally. How many are there, movies where the man, or the actress, apologizes in public? I can't watch them.

"I know," you said.

"I'm *still* mad."

But you'd reached me. Your hands moved to my face and held it. I don't know what I would have done if you'd kissed me but Ed, you knew better. You just held me like that, warm on my teary cheeks. "I know. That's fair."

"Really mad. It's *bad* what you did."

"OK." The crowd was still there but losing interest.

"No, *not* OK," I said, the only fish to fry. "*Yes*. It was *bad*."

"Yes, I'm sorry. I'm sorry."

"Don't say it twenty-six times again. Once was enough."

"Was it?"

"I don't know."

"*Anything*, Min. *Anything*, but tell me what."

"I don't want to tell you anything."

"OK, but *Min, please.*"

"This isn't OK."

"OK, but what can—how can we start?"

"I don't know if I want to."

You blinked fast fast fast. Your hand shivered on my face, and I thought suddenly that now my face was dirty. And, also, that I didn't care. It wasn't OK, Ed, but maybe—

"How, Min? *Anything.* What can I do, what can I—how can I make you want to start?"

I couldn't. No, I thought, do not cry while you're saying it. But then, fuck it, you're crying anyway, and he made you cry. Min, I thought, it's love is what it is. "Coffee," I said, crying. "Coffee, extra cream, three sugars," and you took us away, fast with your arms on me across the field, not a single good-bye to anyone at the Bash, cold through the night to the huddle on the bus, holding my face again, the sweet things you said so soft over the motor, and then marching into In the Cups, pushing the double doors wide slamming open, to proclaim that in penance for mistreating your true love, Min Green, you would like to buy a large coffee, extra cream, three sugars for each and every patron of this fine establishment, which was one bewildered old man with the newspaper who already had a coffee. Insisting that the man be a witness to your solemn promise that never would a drop of Viper touch your lips again. And returning from the bathroom with this tag—

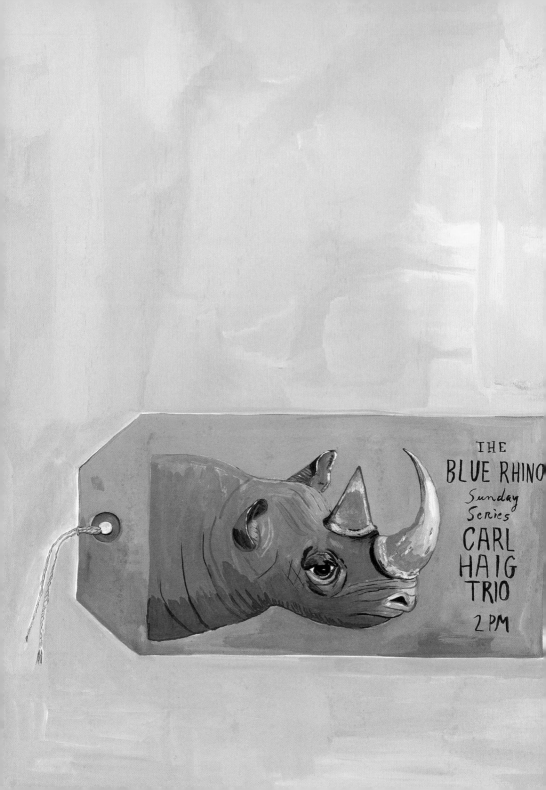

saying, look at this cool tag for a show we *have* to go to tomorrow, because look it's Carl Haig who used to play drums with Hawk Davies who's that guy you and Joanie like, just hanging on the bulletin board like thumbtacked destiny near the bathroom where you'd neatened your hair and buttoned back up decent and sobered, please go with you because you loved me.

"Maybe."

"Oh Min, *please* don't say *maybe* like that."

"OK, yes," I said, as the coffee rolled down inside me. I felt embarrassed, boarding the 6, to still say I was angry about something two buses ago. Trick-or-treaters sat across from us, young with the dad madly scrolling through something on his phone. Total strangers, is what I thought. If I was still mad I was alone, Saturday night, Halloween, on the bus. "Yes, OK? But I'm still mad."

"That's fair," you said, but I didn't want you smiling.

"Still."

"You told me, Min. And I'm still sorry and this is us."

"I know."

"No, our stop, I mean. Time to get off."

And we did, to the cemetery, hushed and welcome in the chilly dark, knowing the Ball was still coming, this stupid bad night. Our feet crackled and trampled on the shadowy grass. "Are you sure you want to go?"

"*Yes*," I said. "My friends—look, I went to your thing."

"OK."

"So you have to suffer through mine. *Anything*, you said."

"Yes, OK."

"And I mean *suffer*. Because I'm still—"

"I know, Min."

I gave you my hand. It was a little less terrible then, just to walk in the quiet. Something rustled, off to one side, but I was safe there, in the dark light on the graves, the crosses of stone, and the dead leaves, almost OK.

"You know," you said, your breath mist, "I thought of this place for the party."

"What?"

"Lottie Carson."

It was the first time you remembered her name. "It's nice," I said.

"But then I realized," you said, "probably insulting, a bad place for an eighty-ninth birthday."

"True," I said. Headlights veered from the street through the trees, the headstones stock-still in the glare, like deer. I could see the numbers of the dates, the life spans long and not long enough. "Maybe she'll be buried here," I said. "We'll have to visit, bring flowers, make sure there aren't any condoms on her grave."

You held my hand tighter, we walked on. You must, Ed, have been thinking about your mom and where, when, she'll end up. You must then, I hope, have meant some of these things you said.

"Maybe *we'll* be buried here," you said, "and our kids will visit with flowers."

"Together," I said, couldn't help whispering. "Together right here."

It was that lovely thing, that time so beautiful there, that led me back to your corner, Ed. We stayed there a minute and then kept walking. The grass was thick, we stopped holding hands, but we were together heading to the rest of the bad night.

The Scandinavian Hall looked like shit, the same old shit with halfhearted streamers fluttering on it. The same gargoyle cooing the same green-lit steam was there at the door like a drunk uncle. We walked in together but nobody noticed because somebody was already fighting, or maybe just a table knocked over, and then with an embarrassed smile you jolted away, desperate for a bathroom. Someone's coat was ruined on a table. I walked blinking, turned aside, past Al, sad in his Pure Evil outfit of a blood-splattered clown, sitting silent with Maria and Jordan, who were dressed as Republicans with oil stains and flag pins. I never told you what happened in the cloakroom. But now I'll tell you because it was nothing. In the cloakroom was the fruit punch in a bowl marked HOPE, but if no chaperones were looking, the boy ladling it out would turn the lazy Susan around, and an identical bowl would come through the curtain with the spiked stuff. And the boy with the ladle was Joe.

"Hey, Min."

"Oh, hi."

"What are you? I know it can't be Hitler, but it looks like it."

I sighed. "A prison warden. I lost my hat. You?"

"My mom. Lost my wig."

"Oh."

"Yeah, oh. Punch? The real stuff?"

"Yes," I said. My insides were wild with coffee and the roller-coaster night. I sat down while he poured it.

"Having a good Halloween?" he asked me.

"Never."

"I'll drink to that."

We clinked plastic cups, unsatisfyingly.

"So how're things?"

"Things?"

"Ed Slaterton, I guess I mean."

"Yeah, I thought you meant that," I said.

"Well, everyone's talking."

"Give me some more punch," I said.

Joe obliged me. That had been the problem. "That well, huh?" he said.

"What?"

"Driving you to drink."

"I guess," I said, drinking and gesturing dramatically. "I'm a basketball widow."

"Is it that bad?"

"No, no. But sometimes. You know, it's a different thing."

"Well, I guess you don't give up at the first sign of trouble," he said, but he wouldn't look at me while I blinked at him.

"Sure I do," I said to him, the closest to sorry I ever got. "What about you? I heard Gretchen Synnit."

"Nope," Joe said. "That was just a cast party. I'm dating Mrs. Grasso now."

"Oh, nice. Though I think gym teachers are usually lesbians."

"Really?"

"Well," I said, "*I've* slept with them all."

"That's why I'm dating Grasso," Joe said. "To get closer to you."

"Shut *up*. You're not missing me."

"Not really," he said. "Though we did say we'd stay friends."

"We're *friends*," I said. "Look, we're having an awkward conversation. If that's not friendship—"

"How about a dance?" he said, and his body teetered to a stand. Very drunk, I realized, but why not? Maybe a dance was what, somewhere for the fury to go. Why not, why the fuck? Why not rise from the grave and terrorize a little instead of staying buried and dead in the cemetery? It was Halloween, and it was "Culture the Vulture" that was booming through the Scandinavian Hall when Joe led me out onto the floor already twirling, the song Joe just loves, the long version we used to listen to on his bedroom floor with shared headphones, my hand resting under his shirt on his smooth belly, driving him crazy, I knew. My unguarded vengeance, unbuttoning my costume for the first time, showing the lining of my dad's forgotten coat and also what I was wearing beneath it. Which had been for you, Ed, just my best bra. Spinning and defiant in my head, flush with punch. And the unbuttoned coat. And Joe's breath against me, sweat I could feel down my neck, the pulse of the second verse. And you, of course, you waiting out the song, self-conscious and stricken, Al too, pretending not to stare, staring, while I danced and pretended not to know. Joe dipping me so low my bra threatened fleshy disaster, I felt my heartbeat beating, brave and fierce, my legs liberated and my arms up in the glorious air, the lights glitter in my eyes, my lips open with the lyrics, and all my thinking erased from my skull while the song roared loud and free. Make it gone, is what I felt. Blow it to hell, kick its ass viciously in high heels, ravish it and rip it up, Ball and Bash both, this cavalcade of battering whatnot, fuck it and let it go. Do it different like they tell you you are. I danced and then I was through, done with every scrap of it, across the floor without looking back, not at Joe now alone, nor Al, nor Lauren, Maria, Jordan, anyone, nobody, everyone else. Just you, the thing worth keeping. The night late, the song over, the singer's last "Madness!" echoing *ness-ness-ness*, and I got to you and met your eyes staring at me in hungry wonder. I knew who you were, Ed Slaterton. I opened my mouth and kissed you then, the first time all night, attacked you and surrendered completely, and let's get out of here. I'm ready, I'm finished, let's not break up, no, no. Take me home, my boyfriend, my love.

And the afternoon after, as bubbly as the stuff they brought us. I met you in front of the Blue Rhino with the sun prickling down on me, a little late because it was hard to find, doubling back around the wrong corner, feeling parched with my limbs moving like gravel had fallen into the machinery, liquor lingering in my body like a song you hate in your head. Inside I wasn't sure—the ceilings were so tall that every sound was an echoey poke at my headache, and the espresso machine kept growling like a wildcat. But the chairs were cool iron, with cushioned backs, and I was comforted and comfortable to sit in them. Pale and haggard, you ordered for us, and they brought this glorious beverage. How did you know about this? Where did it come from, this blessed thing? I never asked you how you knew it or if you knew it and now I'll never know, in fact I have a feeling, I can see it, that if I struggled my way to the Blue Rhino again to find it, there would be no Blue Rhino. It would be a burned-out door maybe, or a brick wall caked with age and grime to show it had been a brick wall forever and the whole safe and sheltered afternoon had been some wish or dream taken back. Like the sad, sad scene in *Sea of Souls* where Ivan Kristeva revisits all the old haunts—*haunts* is how the subtitles put it—and we see that his happiness was some phantom now gone forever, a trick tucked back into its sleeve, only the three playing cards—seven-nine-queen of hearts—proof that he ever met the frightened deposed princess at the peddler's cart, which now sits crumpled and cobwebbed in our hero's stunned gaze. It was a secret time and place, you next to me, untraceable and out of this world.

Carl Haig was so unsteady he had to lean on the arm of a girl I thought was his daughter when he walked to his kit, tottering sunglassed and suited up in a dusty jacket, with hands that looked beaten and brittle even from our corner seats. There was a little applause, and he started fiddling around with the drums and cymbals, just tapping here and there to see what worked or needed fixing. The daughter drank from a tall glass of water, and a guy with a braided beard stepped up and hoisted a tall bass upright just as it became clear Carl was making a beat. The bass started moving some notes around, the cymbals rattled across the ceiling for a sec, and then the two of them were really in gear. I leaned over to rest my head aching on your arm and we sat still for a moment while the music buoyed us along. And then the light hit the waters, and I remembered and lifted mine from our table and took a sip and felt it chilly and fizzy in my throat and my whole body grateful and resurrected just as the girl put down her glass, knelt down low like she was adjusting her shoe, and then stood up tall with a huge golden object in her hands and began to play a deep and lovely melody on the trombone, weird and resonant, fluttering in my ears like the water in my stomach, and I breathed for the first time since Halloween started. Bashes and Balls vanished from memory. I can see it, Ed, I leaned deeper into you, felt you nodding along with the sounds in the room, and your warmth signaled through to me from under your shirt, lovely strong, safe and right. We snuggled up and drank more water, feeling like it had extra oxygen, like we were mineralized and filtered too. Pure, even. And I stretched up to find your ear and whisper it just as you murmured it to me, like we too had practiced together, like we were a combo apart from the frantic of the world, a dotted line sneaking away from the clutch of the school and pressure, just loose and steady beating together in a place nobody else could ever find.

I love you, of course is what we said.

It was just one long song, if song's the word, just some low, calm tones spread out like a banquet in the air, and then it was over and we applauded and headed out the door, with my empty bottle in the pocket of the coat we'd bought to steal sugar, the coat you'd given back to me, the one I'm giving back to you along with everything. I stood outside with you feeling like the Blue Rhino was already fading, that if I didn't say something about what I was feeling right at the moment, then everything would go away and we'd just be in high school again. So I said it.

"I want to give you my keys."

You were smiling, but then you frowned. "What?"

"I said I—"

"What are you talking about? What does that mean?"

I hated my fucking mother. "It just means—"

"It sounds like it means moving in, but Min—"

"Ed—"

"We're in high school. We live with our moms, remember?"

So I had to tell you, in dimwitted humiliation. I had to tell you what I meant, quickly quietly, and once you knew you smiled again. You took my hand and you said you'd take care, you said it, Ed, of everything. You said you'd already found an extraordinary place, and I believed you. I believed you because look at this water, bottled in a place

276

that sounds made up, the odd icons on the label, the way it tasted like nothing, but some kind of better nothing. What does it mean? Where does something like this come from? How can you find it ever again, just what you wanted at just the right time? Never, probably. It's empty and nothing now, I don't even know why I kept it, and I'll keep it no more. It's why we broke up, Ed, a small thing that's disappeared or maybe was never really in my hands in the first place.

The egg cubers, what did you do with the rest of them? Vintage Kitchen had seven and we bought them all, giggling, you even sweaty from practice able to charm a bulk discount from the rectangular mustached man who must have thought we were high. I felt that way, actually, with seven egg cubers in my bag. I took them out, small-talking with a muted Joan on her way out—I should have known then, again—and made an egg-cuber pyramid on the top of the toaster oven while you showered. You must have seen her back out of the driveway through your shutters, because you came down in your towel. We agreed afterward, my hip bruised from the knobs of one of the cupboards, that tomorrow for sure we'd try them out, but then I had to get home, my clothes feeling so loose and messy I was sure my mother could tell they'd been off. Our last *everything but.* In my room I dumped my reluctant homework onto my bed—you can guess just how crucial biology was feeling this month—and found an egg cuber I'd missed. I set it upright on my dresser and then forgot about it until we broke up and the chicken on the box mocked me with its comic-strip complaint. Staring at its own ass, reacting to the cubed egg, the packaging looks so odd and unchanged that Will Ringer probably saw the same thing he calls "a cunning li'l gadget" on page 58 of *Real Recipes from Tinseltown.* The chicken is saying pretty much the short version of this whole letter to you: *?#!* Ouch!*

When Lauren was seven, she saw symbols in a speech balloon, and her super-Christian parents were too God-fearing to explain that the symbols meant *fuck,* so freshman year she had this joke of saying "numbersign questionmark you" and "asterisk exclamationpoint the world." It made me think of her and the alibi. I called her for the first time in forever, as she of course pointed out.

"I know, I know," I said. "I've been busy."

"Yeah. I saw you getting busy at the Ball."

"Shut up."

"It's true. You show up with your basketball superstar and then dance with your ex. Little did I know when we

280

got into *Hands of the Clock* last year that you'd take those soap-opera lessons to heart."

"It was just a dance."

"Just a dance that made Gretchen leave early. And that's not even counting the Al drama. Min, I really wish you guys would, you know, kiss and make up."

"He knows where to find me," I said.

"Yeah," she said sharply. "Basketball practice."

"He's my boyfriend," I said. "That's what he does."

"That and take money from my purse."

"*Lauren*," I said. Lauren and her Bible-sized grudges. Maybe she was the wrong one to ask, I thought.

"I just want you two to be friends again. How are you going to have this movie-star birthday party if we're not invited?"

"*You'll* be invited," I said.

"No, no," she said. "Don't divide and conquer. Al or nothing. Just call him, Min."

"I'll think about it."

"Sure, you'll think about it. *Call him.*"

"OK, OK."

"It's bumming him out and screwing him up. Bonnie Cruz asked him out, and he said he wasn't in a space to think about it, and he hasn't dated since—"

"I know, that girl in LA."

Lauren paused for a sec. "Someday we'll get to that too," she said, like a second-grade teacher about algebra. "But tonight I guess you called to hear me guilt-trip you, right? I mean, there's no other thing, right? Couldn't be."

"Well, I also wanted to hear you sing," I said.

She has this great voice mocking someone at church camp when she was ten. *"Jesus is my dearest flow'r. . . ."*

"OK, OK, mercy. I need a favor."

"His love sustains me through the hours—"

"Lauren!"

"Promise to call Al."

"Yes, yes."

"Swear it."

"I swear it on your mom's Saint Peter statuette."

"Swear it on something holy to *you*."

I wanted to say you. Hawk Davies. "I swear on *The Elevator Descends*."

"OK. Good choice, by the way. Now, what do you need?"

"I need you," I said, "to invite me to sleep over this Saturday."

"Of course," she said, and then "oh."

"Right."

"Like, you won't be here."

"Right."

"But your mom—"

"She'll know I'm with you the whole night."

"Staying over," Lauren said. The line was quiet like an error.

"You'll do it, right?"

"Sounds like *you* will," she said.

"Lauren."

"And answer me this: If I get busted for this—"

"You won't," I said quickly.

"Says *you*, warden."

"You've snuck out before. With *me*. Your parents sleep early and then leave for church before anybody normal gets up."

"And if your suspicious mom calls with some suspicious last-minute thing to check on your suspicious story—"

"She won't."

"Where might I find you when I quickly call you to call her and save my stupid self?"

"She'll call my cell."

"What if she's smarter than a monkey, Min? What then? Where will you be?"

"You can just call me then."

"Min, you want me to be a friend and I am. So tell your friend what is happening."

"Um—"

"Jesus's light always in bloom—"

"Asterisk exclamationpoint," I said, and then told her.

"Oh," she said, slowly, shakily, like she was doing something painful. *Ouch.* Like letting someone down. Like biting her tongue. Like pushing a square egg out of her body. "Oh Min," she said. "I hope you know what you're doing."

283

The pen's dying now. I'll leave it at Leopardi's when I'm done—no, why curse them with my litter? I'll throw it into the box when I'm through with you, like movie thugs who run out of bullets and toss the gun. These last faint pages will be like this photo, a lost and blurry piece of old-fashioned magic capturing an image of a thing unclear, almost legendary. Nobody else made one probably, no matter what the stars say, and now there's only this bad trace of ours I'm reminding you of, in fading ink. It's like we never had anything.

We got off the bus early and bought the eggs and cheap caviar and the British cucumber and one big tough lemon.

You told me a story of Joan buying a lot of cucumbers years ago, by mistake, to make zucchini bread, and that reminded me to ask you and *your whole household*, her words, from my mom to Thanksgiving. I didn't add all the things *she* said, how the holidays must be so difficult etc., but I told you Joan could come cook. I told you we had to do it sometime, get you and your mom and me and my mom in the same room. I said maybe it wouldn't be so bad, nice even. We talked about which Thanksgiving foods absolutely had to be made the same way every year, the traditionals, and which had room for experimentation and improvement. We didn't agree much, and for some reason this time it was weird.

You said maybe.

At your house you showered and I boiled water. I lowered the eggs in like I'd learned from Joan with the Burmese soup, but Joan wasn't there to approve. So it was just silent, the water off upstairs and no music in the kitchen because I knew you didn't like Hawk Davies and you'd already been a good sport with the Blue Rhino, so I put on nothing and waited for the eggs. You came down fully dressed and started slicing the cucumber and kissed me on the top of my head. I stayed there loving you, though the love made me, not sad but I guess melancholy, for a reason I couldn't point to. I tried to perk up reading enthusiastic from the cookbook, but it was actually a very simple thing to do. Instructions were superfluous. We smiled stuffing the eggs into the cubers but didn't laugh, put everything in the fridge, and then it was time to wait. We lay on the sofa. The TV clicked and flopped. We got up, put the second batch in, sat back down. The afternoon stayed saggy. My stomach felt in a fistfight, even with your hands around me and the kisses at my ear. The timer went off again and we got to work, me eating the hard-boiled scraps as we assembled, which didn't help my stomach any. You had it drawn out already in a Calc II sketch, your lines straight and protracted, your knife-work sharp on the curves. And then we had it, pushing the last touches into place. We beheld it like astronauts, our hands afraid to get any closer. It was magic, but it was weirder than it was magic, exactly what we'd planned, the perfect thing I'd found in the book actually there in the smooth white flesh, but still so strange. I thought, I couldn't help it, of what Lauren said. Did we know what we were doing?

We were still standing Frankenstein looking at it when Joan came in clutching textbooks and artichokes. "Hey," she said. "What is that in my kitchen?"

"*Our* kitchen," you said.

"Who's making dinner tonight," she said, taking off a scarf I loved, "and every night? *Us?* In *our* kitchen? Or *me?*"

"This," I said, enough of the Slaterton Sibling Bickerfest, "is—"

"Wait, I know what it is," Joan said. "This is the igloo thing you told me about, Min. You actually made it."

"It's Greta's Cubed-Egg Igloo on an ice floe of lemon-pickled cucumber with a caviar surprise."

Joan put down her bags. "What's the caviar surprise?"

"There's caviar in it," I said.

"Inside there?"

"Inside the igloo, yes."

"And it's all—*eggs*?"

"We cubed them and then set them up. What do you think?"

Joan cocked her head at it. "I don't know what to think," she said. "I mean, it's sort of awesome."

"Good for a party?" I asked.

"The guests would have to be tiny to get inside."

"*Joan*," you said.

"And what are those things lined up drying?"

"Egg cubers," I said. "We had to buy a bunch."

"I'm sure that's an investment you'll never regret," she said.

"*Joanie.*"

"Well, we'll make another one for the real party," I said. "This is just a trial run."

"The birthday party thing, I'm remembering," she said.

"*Real Recipes from Tinseltown*," I said. "It's Will Ringer's recipe, inspired by *Greta in the Wild*."

"You said you were going to make an igloo for Lottie Carson's eighty-ninth birthday," she said in wonder, "and then you did, just like you wanted. Just like you said, I mean. Wow."

You stood there grinning in a small way.

"Let me get my camera," she said. "Can I take a picture?"

"Sure," I said.

"This sort of thing," she said, her voice serious with lingering disbelief, "should be documented."

She bounded upstairs and we were alone in the kitchen. After a stretched-out silence we both started talking. I was going to say something stupid and you said—

"Sorry, what?"

"No, you go."

"But—"

"Really."

You took my hand. "I was just going to say that I know it's been weird, this afternoon. Awkward."

"Yeah," I said.

"But I think it'll be better, you know, after," you said. "Tomorrow, I mean."

"I know what you mean," I said.

"Sorry."

"No, I think you're right."

"I love you."

"I love you too."

"And you know," you said, "you can, it's not a big deal if you change your mind."

I leaned against you, hard, like I'd forgotten how to stand

for just a sec. "I won't," I said, and it was true. But it was just true *then*. "I'll never change my mind."

We stayed like that listening to Joan close a closet and come down. Ed, it's ridiculous, but I loved her too. And could goddamn kill her for not saying something. Though what she could have said that I could have heard I cannot for the life of me see.

"I'm using the Insta-Deluxe," she said to Ed. "Remember? We have shoe boxes full of us from this. Old-fashioned I know, they probably don't make them anymore. But digital didn't seem good enough for something like this."

"They still make them," I said. "They got trendy for a while after that scene in *Sinister Development*."

She took the picture with a whir and the gears of antiquated stuff. The picture came out of the slot, and she shook it so the fog would clear quicker. "So what are your big Friday night plans?" she asked us, *shake shake shake*. "Ooh, I know. Eating a big igloo."

I shook my head. "Can't. I have sort of a family thing."

"Oh," Joan said, with a sideways look at you. You'd told me you had better stay home, Ed, if you fucking remember. "Well, I'm celebrating my last midterm on the sofa with fried artichokes and garlic aioli and *The Sand on the Beach*."

"That's supposed to be amazing," I said, but you were already taking my hand, so I didn't say what I wanted, *Wish I could stay*.

"And when I'm gone tomorrow night," Joan said sternly, "I expect only a limited amount of hanky-panky from you two."

"Min already has a mother," you said. "Don't be hers, Joan. Plus, we're just going out." This was not a lie.

"OK, OK," she said. "You're right. Her mother will make sure, from what I hear. But I had to say something, Ed."

"I'll see you tomorrow," you said, like you did too. "I'll call you in the morning."

"I love you," I said, in front of your sister, and you kissed my cheek.

"Don't forget your picture," Joan said quickly, so you wouldn't have to say anything, I guess. She put this in my hand. We all walked toward the door and stopped for another sec to look at the igloo and then the photo and then the igloo again. It was better in real life than looking at it now, bigger in the kitchen, more grand, like a fantastic something you could walk into, a princess castle, a dream come true. Here it just looks strange. It was strange. But I loved it too.

"Why do *I* have the picture?" I said. "You're the one who said it should be documented."

"You keep it, Min," Joan said quietly. She said, "You dreamed it up," or something. She said it was my idea. And then she said something like, keep it in case it doesn't work the next time. Keep this, in case it doesn't work when you try it again.

help us
SAVE the PLANET
A TOWEL ON THE FLOOR
MEANS PLEASE GIVE ME MORE.
A TOWEL ON THE RACK
MEANS NO LACK

I don't know why this is the part I kept, this thing that was on the towel rack. It seems gross a little, like a reminder that they *did* have to change the linens after all. If I could have chosen anything, it would have been something from the lounge part of Dawn's Early Lite Lounge and Motel, where I'd been once freshman year after a synagogue dance this guy Aram took me to. Aram and I had tall ginger ales and stared up at the ceiling of the lounge, taxidermy birds dusty in a circle along the molding, with a huge butterfly in the very center, flapping slowly slowly slowly with motorized fans for wings, and speakers playing nature sounds.

It *is* extraordinary, Ed. I'll give you that. Even the big sign outside, the *Lite* lit up and flashing, is glamorous and attractive with those three arrows taking turns illuminating so the arrow is moving, leading everyone on South Ninth to the parking lot behind. It's probably the most extraordinary place we have. You thought hard and found it, Ed, the place to take me.

But I didn't want to go to the lounge. You said there was no rush but there *was*, we'd already pushed dumplings around at Moon Lake, pretending it was only another date. I ate maybe three bites. The whole night I tasted snow peas in my nervous mouth. Plus maybe somebody would see us in the lounge. I waited in the car while you brought back the keys.

The motel was laid out in curves and balconies at the edge of the vast lot. It probably looked like something from the air, I could see it in an aerial angle like a still in *When the Lights Go Down* as we crossed the dark asphalt with our bags. "Establishing shot," is what the caption would say, "from *The Moron Who Thought Love Was Forever*."

The room looked like a room, not extraordinary. The curtains closed with a long plastic wand like something Mika Harwich uses on the horses in *Look Me in the Eye*. The desk was flimsy, the hair dryer tiny as a revolver on the bathroom wall. There was a plastic globe plugged into a corner socket brand-named Spring in the Air that smelled like a violated flower. I went down the hallway to get ice and found next to the machine some empty cardboard boxes stacked up loosely, all from furniture. TWO WOODEN HEADBOARDS it said on one. ONE FLOOR LAMP. I swear, ONE NIGHT STAND.

"I can't make this work," you said when I got back. You'd turned the TV around like you were giving it a haircut, fiddling with the plugs and holes and whatnot, looking for a connection.

"What are you doing?"

"Getting ready to film it, of course," you said.

I must not have looked like I knew you were kidding.

"A movie. I was supposed to be able to play it through the computer. I thought it'd be nice."

"What movie?"

"*When the Smoke Clears*," you said, "from Joan's collection. It sounded, you know, like something you'd like. And me too. These people, a soldier and a veterinarian meet in the war, out in the country I guess, it said in the description—"

"It's good," I said quietly. I put the ice down but kept my hands leaning on it. On the dresser were two small bottles, a beer for you and white wine from Australia, shipped or flown I thought, around the world. *All the way.*

"Oh, you've seen it."

"Part of it. A long time ago."

"Well, we can still watch it on the laptop."

"It's OK."

"Oh."

"I mean, maybe."

"There's strawberries too," you said, lifting an eager container out of your backpack. I thought, you'd thought of everything.

"How'd you find strawberries in November?" I took them to rinse in the sink.

"There's this place over on Nosson. It's only open for ten minutes Wednesdays at four AM."

"Shut up."

"I love you."

I saw me in the yellowy mirror. "I love you too."

When I came back out, you'd changed the lighting somehow, though the bedspread was still ugly, nothing to be done. I put down the dripping berries. Your shoulders shrugged up underneath your shirt, I couldn't wait to see them again, beautiful things. *Extraordinary*. And I looked you in your eyes, wide and lit with fondness and mischief and lust. For me, like me. I had such, you would not believe the such a feeling I had. You couldn't film it, it couldn't be captured. It couldn't happen almost, but there it was happening anyway. I kicked off my shoes, biting my lip because I might have laughed. I was thinking of something Coach always said to you and your team at practice while I watched. *OK people*, he said sometimes, *let's get right to it*.

Criminy, I remember you saying. I was smiling because I didn't have to be guided like I thought I'd be, not as much. I could do some things. Some parts I was very good at.

"Was that time better?" you said.

"It's supposed to hurt," I said.

"I know," you said, and put both hands on me. "But, I guess I mean, but what is it like?"

"Like putting a whole grapefruit into your mouth."

"You mean it's tight?"

"No," I said, "I mean it doesn't fit. Have you ever tried to put a whole grapefruit into your mouth?"

The laughing was the best part.

LiKE iT WAS ALL NORMAL

And then late at night we were starving, remember? "Room service?" I said.

"Let's not push our luck, we're paying cash," you said, and found a phone book. "Pizza."

"Pizza." I was fierce with the thought of it. My first grown-up meal, I couldn't help thinking, and what I want is kid stuff.

I was bashful and hid in the bathroom when it was delivered. I listened to you talk normally to the guy and even laugh at something, like it was all normal, standing in a T-shirt and boxers in the doorway, taking the pizza with the dollars in change on top while I huddled by the sink running this through my hair. I felt like I was over by a pole, a bicycle or a dog, while the owner chatted oblivious and relaxed. It was your ease, I realized, your ease and expertise that made me nauseous. I grabbed the comb, the cardboard message on the rack, like I was hiding shameful evidence. I'd never felt something like this, but you'd done it all before.

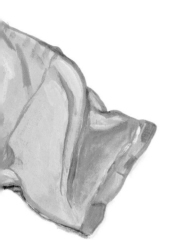

My first pizza bite sent sauce squirting onto my top, and it looked so bloodlike I had to take it off. You gave me this, another one of the astonishing number of items in your bottomless backpack, and I slept wearing it next to you, and then nights and nights at home, so long on me it felt like I was inside you, stretched down your tall legs and curled up in your chest where your heart beat. Which I guess made us even. We kissed so tender when we woke up, never mind our sour breath and the bedspread even uglier by day. But we had to run for coffee before Lauren called or anyone found out. It was already afternoon, a disapproving gray in the sky. "I love you too," I remember saying, so it must have been a reply, you must have said it first, but even now, looking at this shirt, I try not to think or picture anything at all. I wore this, Ed, is what I think, like shelter and skin, that night alone on the roof of the garage. The bed felt too empty to sleep, so I was out in the night lighting some of those matches, Mayakovsky's Dream feeling decades ago, the tiny fires dying out in the wind as soon as they left my hands. Cold, for no reason. Hot, for no reason. Smiling, crying, nothing at all, this shirt my only company that night and so many nights after. I wore it, this careless thing you don't even remember giving to me from your bag. It wasn't a gift, this thing I'm returning. It was barely a gesture, almost forgotten already, this thing I wore like it was dear to me. And it was. No wonder we broke up.

OK, these were a gift, waiting in my locker Monday. But now you had my combination, so you could do things like this. So ugly, or not ugly, really, but wrong for me. I don't like to think about, Will! Not! Goddamn! Think about! who helped you pick them out. Or what were you thinking. Look at them, dangling stupid. What *were* you thinking?

NAPOLI - VESUVIO

Take these relics too. Al just told me where he got them, at Bicycle Stationery, in one of those big baskets they lug out front like some snake-charming's going to happen. But when he put them in my hands that morning, he didn't tell me that. There was too much else to tell. He'd been sitting on the right-side bench, our usual spot, which I hadn't touched since you and I had started smacking my life around. It looked like a relic, too, relicky Al with relicky Lauren and a spot for me grave-robbed empty.

It was a wonder I was there, so lost in quavery thought

that I'd forgotten to enter Hellman the new way, to wave at you shooting hoops and maybe even kiss a little through the chain-link fence like separated prisoners. But there I was, and Al walked to meet my walking. Even after ten days, girls probably do walk different after virginity, just because we think everyone can tell.

"What are these?"

"I swore to Lauren that I'd talk to you," Al said, "and I know you swore too."

"What'd you swear on?" I said.

"Gina Vadia in *Three True Liars*."

"Good one," I said, although I knew it was just because of the sports car.

"How about you?"

"The Elevator Descends."

"Nice."

"Yeah."

"But you didn't call," he said.

"Well," I said, turning the bundle around in my hands, "I thought I should communicate by postcard instead, but I don't have any. Oh, look."

"They're invitations, I thought," Al said. "For the party."

"You're still," I said, "helping with it?"

"I don't think Lottie Carson should suffer just because we had a fight." He was talking in his perfect deadpan, but his face was wary, almost desperate. Behind him Lauren walked slowly backward away, watching us both like we were a dangerous climb. "Look at them."

I flipped through without untying. "Wow, volcanoes."

"Perfect, right? Because of her in *The Fall of Pompeii*?"

"Sure."

"I mean, if we're going to honor her right."

"Yeah, thanks. Ed and I were saying that we should invite her first, make sure she doesn't have other plans. I want to take her flowers, do it in person."

"Really?"

"Well, I'm nervous about it," I said. "Maybe I'll just write a card." I swallowed a long slow swallow of nothing. "Thanks, Al. These are cool."

"Sure. What's the use of friendship?"

"Right, OK."

"Listen, Min." Al put his hands so deep in his pockets I thought I'd never see them again. "I don't think you and Ed—"

My hand closed on the postcards. "Don't, don't, *don't* say anything about Ed. He's not whatever you think he is."

"It's not that. I don't have any opinion of him."

"Please."

"I don't. That's what I'm saying. What I said, the things about him I said—what I'm saying is that there's a reason I said them."

"Because you don't like him," I said, never in the world

317

thinking I would talk in this tone to my friend Al. "I get it."

"Min, I don't know him. It's not about Ed is what I mean."

"Then what—?"

"There's a reason."

"Well," I said, sick of this shit, "then tell me the reason. Stop secreting around about it."

Al looked behind me, at the ground, everywhere else. "I swore to Lauren I would tell you this," he said quietly, and then, "*Jealousy*—OK?—is why."

"*Jealousy?* You wish you played basketball?"

He sighed. "Don't be an idiot," he said, "and it would make it easier."

"I'm *not*. Ed—"

"—is with you," Al finished for me, of course. The school got wider, the whole place. There are so many movies like this, where you thought you were smarter than the screen but the director was smarter than you, *of course* he's the one, *of course* it was a dream, *of course* she's dead, *of course* it's hidden right there, *of course* it's the truth and you in your seat have failed to notice in the dark. I could see them all, every reveal that ever surprised me, but I could not see this one, or know how I could not have known.

"Oh," I said, or something.

Al gave me a smile of, *what can you do?* "Yeah."

"I guess I *am* an idiot."

"One of us is," Al said simply. "There's nothing idiotic about not thinking about me that way, Min. Most people don't."

"That girl in LA," I said. "Oh." *Of course*, again. "Whose idea was that?"

"That movie *Kiss Me, Fool*."

"But that's a terrible movie."

"Yeah, well, it didn't work, making that up," Al said. "You didn't get jealous."

"She sounded nice," I said wistfully.

"I just," Al said, "described you."

Then *where were you*, is what I wanted to say, *all my lonely times*, but right next to me, I knew, was where. "Why didn't you tell me?"

"Would it have mattered?"

I sighed shakily at the end of my rope. I said a thing, made some noise, in order not to say *probably*.

"Well, I'm telling you now, I guess."

"Now that I'm in love."

"You aren't," Al said, "the only one."

It was a true heart he had, Ed. *Has*, still, leaving to pull his truck around so I can finish. But that morning—November 12—I didn't have a place to put it, I could hardly hold these postcards of old dangers and disasters. I was blinking, I knew, too many times. In a sec the bell was going to ring.

"It's a lot, I know," Al said. "And you don't have to, you know, feel the same or anything."

"I can't," I said.

"Yes, then, don't do anything," he said. "That's fine too, Min. Really. But let's stop, like, *scowling* at each other and not talking. Let's have coffee."

I was shaking my head. "I have a test," I said stupidly.

"Well, not now. But *sometime*. You know, at Federico's. We haven't in forever."

"Sometime," I said, not quite in agreement, but Al said "OK" and lifted one foot like he does, balance-beamy, like there was a part of the place we had to be careful on.

"OK," I said too.

He looked like he wanted to say something else. He should have. I didn't want him to. It wouldn't have mattered. "OK, though? Is it?"

"OK," I said again, and again, and then I said I had to go.

Here we are at the bottom, almost empty. It's like confetti, these dried remnants you find in the street for a party no one invited you to. But they used to be, I can admit, part of something beautiful.

Lauren told me when we hung out that weekend that you must have wanted to be found out, that you wanted it over and that's why we ended up at Willows after practice. I think and think about it. But what I think is you were just outmaneuvered. I'd seen it happen at games, suddenly the others upon you and the ball gone the sec your eyes wandered, the very moment of distraction. When you were cocky sometimes it happened, or not enough sleep. "God I need coffee," you told me, out of the gym. "Extra cream, three sugars."

I, the idiot, waved at Annette and took your arm to walk you away. "On the way to Willows," I said.

"What? Not home?"

"Joan's getting tired of me," I said. "Plus I want to go to Lottie Carson's place. Today's the day to invite her."

"OK, all the way out there," you said, "but why Willows? You said you never wanted flowers."

"They're for her," I said. "Then we can have coffee at Fair Grounds while I write to her on one of these."

"One of whats?"

"Look. Cool, huh? She was in a volcano movie."

"Where'd you get these?"

"Al got them."

"So you guys are better now?"

"Yeah, we're OK."

"Good. He must be getting laid, he was getting too crazy Todd says, even in class. That girl from LA come out for a visit?"

"Long story," I said.

You nodded dismissively and then remembered you were supposed to listen to such things. "Tell me over coffee," you said.

"Flowers first."

"Min, I don't know. Flowers? Why?"

"Because she's a movie star," I said, "and we're, like, high school kids."

"Let's have coffee and talk about it."

"No, you told me Willows closes early."

"Yeah," you admitted, good at math. "That's why I said coffee first."

"*Ed.*"

"*Min.*"

We stood cross at one another but knowing, at least me, it was another cute bicker. "You still aren't wearing the earrings," you said, like this might get you your way.

"I told you," I said. "They're fancy, kind of."

"That's not what she said when I bought them."

"She who?"

"I don't know," you goddamn stammered. "The jewelry store lady."

"Well, they are. We can go somewhere fancy, then I'll wear them." This was a hint, I wish I didn't have to admit, that you would ask me to the Holiday Formal. You hadn't, you didn't, you are swine. "Right now, though, it's Willows. Come on."

I dragged you, sweaty and wriggling, down the two or three blocks, your legs moving in a choppy tiptoe like you had to pee, some exaggerated dance that still spelled out grace. Your hand squirmy in mine like a caught frog, your hair needing cutting, your lips bitten and wet. Wish it was the last time I found you beautiful, Ed. I could have let you go then, pushed back your kisses and toppled us into traffic instead of the way you haunt my hallways now. I should have had a feeling right then, in the last crosswalk as the light changed, because instead—

The Willows door beeped open. Inside was a hothouse of choices among which you hemmed and shrugged. "What does it mean?" I asked. "You've done more flowers than I have."

"Um."

"Though I guess not in a while, huh? These are pretty. Lily."

"Um."

"Some of these are so lovely I never should have said the thing about flowers. I should have fought with you and fought with you just to get them."

"Um."

"Do you do them in that old-fashioned code, like daffodils mean *I'm sorry I was late*, daisies mean *sorry I embarrassed you in front of your friends*, these things here fanned out mean *just thinking of you*? Or did you just have them throw whatever was pretty together?" I was a stupid marionette in there, spritely and thinking I was cute when all the while it was a jerky joke even kids found tedious. "What's the one for *happy birthday*? Or *please come to our party*? What's flower code for *you don't know me but if you are who we think you are, we love your work and my boyfriend and I have been organizing an elegant affair for your eighty-ninth, please come? How do you say make my dreams come true?*"

"You must be Annette."

No, that wasn't it.

"How are you, Ed?" the flower guy said, bald with glasses on a necklace of beads. I told myself he hadn't said that or I hadn't heard him or I was not hearing you staying silent, even as he shook my hand. "So nice to put a name to a face finally."

"No, Ambrose," you said finally. "We're just looking for—"

"I know what you're looking for," he said in a wavery coo, and crossed to a wall of fridges. "Saving me the delivery charges. I'll knock ten bucks off your mother's account, Ed. Do you know his mother, Annette?" He shut the door and walked toward me in a flashing shrub of scarlet. "She's loved flowers forever," he said, and placed it in my hands, sparkling, an impressive arrangement, tall in a vase chilly in my hand. Red roses. Everybody knows what that means.

"Those aren't for her," you said suddenly, and this was also, Ed, the wrong goddamn thing.

"You're not Annette?"

Annette, it was still taking me a sec. It was the name on the little envelope, offered up on a plastic spear like a spit in my face. For a girlfriend, red roses would have to be, and that was me. So I took it, the envelope cold too, and sharp on the edges.

"No," you said quietly.

Ed, they were very, very beautiful to see.

"I'd like to see," I found myself lying, "what you wrote to—" I'd already scraggled it open. The gasp in the room must have been, embarrassing, mine.

I can't stop thinking about you.

It was an ocean, a canyon of awful. I couldn't see it, some scene in a flower shop. Stop gulping, is what I thought to myself. Your expression is moronic in the reflection of the glass door. And now she's going to say, I'd predict scornfully sitting through this movie at home, *How long has this been going on?*

And I said it.

"Min—"

"I mean, it seems like *awhile*," I said, the word slimy in my mouth, "because, I mean, you can't stop thinking of her." The florist put his hand on his face. All the gay talk, I had time to think, and look who knows your boy-girl secrets, Ed.

"Min, I was trying to tell you."

"But this isn't for me," I said, and something crinkled in my fist. There was a crash on the floor, the crash of letting something go.

"Min, I love you."

"And you can't stop thinking of me," I said, "is what it was in your note." My head rattled with bad arithmetic. You must have stopped thinking of me because you couldn't stop with Annette. I thought of her in the chains, the ax, and closed my fist around those goddamn petals right here. *Couldn't stop thinking of who*, I thought, a fraction I couldn't add up in my head. I needed help, but you're the only one good with a fucking protractor.

"Min, listen—"

"I am!" I shouted. "Listening!" I threw the envelope— *now she's going to throw the envelope in his face*—in your face. "Are you—when did—"

"Look, first of all I never said we wouldn't see other people."

"*Bullshit!*" I said. "We said that very thing!"

"I said I didn't *want* to see anybody else," you said, back on the noisy bus, for a sec it was Halloween and I felt the night air on my arms, "not that—"

"*Bullshit!* You said you loved me!"

"I do, Min, but Annette, you know, she lives right nearby. And you know we've stayed friends. I mean, you have guy friends, you know how it is, and I've never given you a hard time about it—"

"She *lives nearby*?"

"So she'd come over some nights, just for homework

or whatever. She never got on with Joan, so we'd always be upstairs."

"Oh God."

"She likes basketball, Min. I don't know. Her dad used to be friends with mine. She's a good listener. And yes, mostly it was just friends."

"You—did you sleep with her?" Nights I began to add up, when we didn't talk on the phone, or did but quickly. Joan mad and evasive answering, stomping upstairs to fetch you. I was a good listener, I am one. I was listening to all of it. But now, then, you didn't say anything. Just the water rivering on the floor, an answer I knew, gone out of the pretty vase.

"Look, Min, I know you don't believe me, but this is hard. For me too. It's awful, it's weird, it's like I was two people and one of them was, yes, Min, *really*—really really happy with you. I did love you, I do. But then at night Annette would knock on my window and it was just like something else, like a secret *I* didn't even know about—"

The room rattled, the glass doors of the fridge. You stopped talking. I must have screamed, I thought.

"Min, *please.* It was—we're—it's *different*, you know that." You had the same look from the court again, thinking quick strategy. "There must be some—I don't know, like a movie, right? Isn't there some movie where it's like there's two guys, twins I think, one guy doing the right thing and—"

"This isn't a movie," I said. "We're not movie stars. We're—oh my God. *Oh my God.*"

I was staring at something else now, *staring.* How many, I wondered, terrible things would be projected in front of me, bad scenes in worse movies, stupid mistakes, how many travesties that had to be torn off the walls?

"Hey," said the flower guy. "Wait."

I shook my wrist out of his hand and kept ripping. I'd tear it all down, I thought, wreck whatever the fuck I wanted and anyone who tried to stop me. "Wait," the guy said again, "wait. I realize you're upset and, well, part of it is *my* fault. But you can't vandalize my store. That's *mine*, dear. She always meant the world to me and I'll never find that again if you—"

I ran out with both hands full roaring. Nobody on the sidewalk cared. The air was too cold, like I'd forgotten my coat, and then unbearably close and hot in my mouth, my body. You came after me. My fucking virginity, I realized with a churning lurch. You had seen everything, you had everything. Showering together. Your body inside mine. You had every scrap of skin, and I had a handful of petals in one hand, somebody else's flowers, and this in the other. How many times had you been in Willows, seen it right there tacked to the wall next to a picture of kittens hanging from a tree, all bug-eyed sad, with a stupid caption everybody's seen a million times?

"Did you know about this?" I stormed at you.

You gave another fury-making shrug. "Min, I didn't understand—"

"*I* don't understand," I said, trying to *hang in there*. "Are you—did you dump me for another girl and I didn't even know it?"

You blinked like maybe it was a close guess.

"And then this? *This?* And you never—"

"You're the one," you said, "Min, who said, you always said *even if it isn't*! You said that *even if it isn't*—"

"You knew and didn't tell me?"

Nothing from you.

"Tell me!"

"I don't know," you said. Beautiful in the dimming sun. I could have touched you, wanted to, couldn't stand it. Who were you, Ed? What could I do with you?

"What's the other choice?" I cried. "What else is there?"

"Min, it's different," you said, but I was shaking my head so violently. "You *are*! You're—"

"Don't fucking say *arty*! I'm not arty!"

"—different" which was what shattered me. I fled down the street because it was not true. It *wasn't*. It wasn't and it isn't. You're a goddamn athlete and could have caught me without breaking a sweat but, Ed, you didn't, you weren't there when I reached a far lost corner and stood heaving with my hands full of all I had left. It wasn't true, Ed, I was

334

going to scream it at you when you called my name, but you were gone, it wasn't you. Of all people Jillian Beach was there, in that car her dad bought her shiny with bumpers and bad music at the red light. She was my best friend, Ed, is how fucking low you threw me to. She just opened her passenger door, and I sobbed everywhere. She turned off the radio, of all people, and didn't ask anything. Later it came to me seeing her avoid my gaze at the lockers that she must have already known what it meant to find me there alone sobbing, that I'd finally found out. But then it just seemed magic and gratefully extraordinary that she said nothing and let me cry desperate and ugly in her car, drove calmly where she knew I needed to go, and then stopped. She reached across me and opened the door. She gave me my bag even with my hands full and, Ed, a kiss, even, a kiss on my weepy cheek. A little push. I was hiccuping now, it couldn't be worse, but I saw what she meant and stumbled through the door. The few people looked up at the girl crying, and Al rose from the table where we always sit at Federico's if we can, his face pale and grave while I cried and cried and told him the truth of it.

And the truth is that I'm *not*, Ed, is what I wanted to tell you. I'm not different. I'm not arty like everyone says who doesn't know me, I don't paint, I can't draw, I play no instrument, I can't sing. I'm not in plays, I wanted to say, I don't write poems. I can't dance except tipsy at dances.

I'm not athletic, I'm not a goth or a cheerleader, I'm not treasurer or co-captain. I'm not gay and out and proud, I'm not that kid from Sri Lanka, not a triplet, a prep, a drunk, a genius, a hippie, a Christian, a slut, not even one of those super-Jewish girls with a yarmulke gang wishing everyone a happy Sukkoth. I'm not anything, this is what I realized to Al crying with my hands dropping the petals but holding this too tight to let go. I like movies, everyone knows I do—I love them—but I will never be in charge of one because my ideas are stupid and wrong in my head. There's nothing different about that, nothing fascinating, interesting, worth looking at. I have bad hair and stupid eyes. I have a body that's nothing. I'm too fat and my mouth is idiotic ugly. My clothes are a joke, my jokes are desperate and complicated and nobody else laughs. I talk like a moron, I can't say one thing to talk to people that makes them like me, I just babble and sputter like a drinking fountain broken. My mother hates me, I can't please her. My dad never calls and then calls at the wrong time and sends big gifts or nothing, and all of it makes me scowl at him, and he named me Minerva. I talk shit about everybody and then sulk when they don't call me, my friends fall away like I've dropped them out of an airplane, my ex-boyfriend thinks I'm Hitler when he sees me. I scratch at places on my body, I sweat everywhere, my arms, the way I clumsy around dropping things, my average grades and stupid interests, bad breath, pants tight in back, my neck too long or something. I'm sneaky and get caught, I'm snobby and faking it, I agree with liars, I say whatnot and think that's some clever thing. I have to be watched when I cook so I don't burn it down. I can't run four blocks or fold a sweater. I make out like an imbecile, I fool around foolishly, I lost my virginity and couldn't even do that right, agreeing to it and getting sad and annoying afterward, clinging to a boy everyone knows is a jerk bastard asshole prick, loving him like I'm fucking twelve and learning the whole of life from a smiley magazine. I love like a fool, like a Z-grade off-brand romantic comedy, a loon in too much makeup saying things in an awkward script to a handsome man with his own canceled comedy show. I'm not a romantic, I'm a half-wit. Only stupid people would think I'm smart. I'm not something anyone should know. I'm a lunatic wandering around for scraps, I'm like every single miserable moron I've scorned and pretended I didn't recognize. I'm all of them, every last ugly thing in a bad last-minute costume. I'm not different, not at all, not different from any other speck of a thing. I'm a blemished blemish, a ruined ruin, a stained wreck so failed I can't see what I used to be. I'm nothing, not a single thing. The only particle I had, the only tiny thing raising me up, is that I was Ed Slaterton's girlfriend, loved by you for like ten secs, and who cares, so what, and not anymore so how embarrassing for me. How wrong to think I was anyone else,

337

like thinking grass stains make you a beautiful view, like getting kissed makes you kissable, like feeling warm makes you coffee, like liking movies makes you a director. How utterly incorrect to think it any other way, a box of crap is treasures, a boy smiling means it, a gentle moment is a life improved. It's not, it isn't, catastrophic to think so, a pudgy toddler in a living room dreaming of ballerinas, a girl in bed star-eyed over *Never by Candlelight*, a nut thinking she is loved following a stranger in the street. There is not a movie star walking by, is what I know now, don't follow her thinking so, don't be ridiculously wrong and dream of an eighty-ninth birthday party celebrating feebleminded smattering ignorance. It's gone. She died a long time ago, is the real truth of what slayed me in my chest and head and hands forever. There are no stars in my life. When Al dropped me home, exhausted and raw, to climb out over the garage and realize it all over again crying alone, there weren't even stars in the sky. The last of the matches was the only light, all I had, and then those, those you gave me you bastard, those were dead and nothing too.

ACTRESS LOTTIE CARSON

Not a single spider mum could be found in the florist shops in Hollywood today as Lottie Carson, one of the brightest stars of Hollywood's Golden Age, was laid to rest in a private cemetery on the property of famed film director P. F. Mailer. The spider mum became Carson's signature flower following her startling debut in what was otherwise a standard programmer, Spider Mum Flapper. Though Carson had but a bit part, audiences the world over were entranced by her unforgettable face and her dance number, "A Nose for News," in which Carson and twelve Quiglerettes formed a human face by undulating their tuxedoed bodies in a dance that ended up as a key piece of evidence in a famed U.S. Supreme Court case.

Born Bettina Vaporetto in Buffalo, New York, Carson was the daughter of two Italian immigrants known locally for domestic brawls that left them swinging pans—both Vincent and Angelina Vaporetto were ranked amateur fencers—in the streets at all hours of the day and night.

cont. D 8

— DEAD AT SEVENTY-FIVE

An early promotional still of Carson, with one of her famed spider mums in her teeth.

I bought this but didn't use it. Al and Lauren kidnapped me to make wild-mushroom lasagna and cry at the table instead of hiding in the nonreserved seats to watch you play, like I told them I wanted to.

"Have some dignity," Lauren said to me, and Al nodded in agreement over the cheese grater. "You don't want to be that sad ex-girlfriend in the stands."

"I am that sad ex-girlfriend in the stands," I said.

"No, you're here with us," Al said firmly.

"That's all I am," I said, "or having dinner with my mother all sullen, or crying on my bed, or staring at the phone —"

"Oh, Min."

"—or listening to Hawk Davies and throwing him away and fishing him out of the trash and listening to him more and going through the box again. There's nothing else. I'm—"

"The box?" Al said. "What's the box?"

I bit my lip. Lauren gasped. "I know," I said. "I know, I know, I should have broken up with him on Halloween."

"What's the box?" Al said again.

Lauren leaned down to look me in the eye. "You do not," Lauren said, "tell me you don't have a box of stuff, of Ed Slaterton *treasures* you've been pawing through. God in heaven, no. Did I not tell you, Al? Didn't I say we should have searched her room with a fine-tooth comb and torched every Slaterton thing we could find? From the moment we learned about his scummy, *scummy* behavior we should have gone and rented some of those radiation suits and para-trooped into her room—"

But she stopped because I was crying, and Al took off his apron and came over to hug me. At least, I thought, I'm not crying as hard as the last time. "It's stupid, I know," I said. "It's desperate stupid. *I'm* desperate stupid. I'm a desperado for keeping all of it."

"When it's a girl," Al said, handing me a napkin, "I believe the term is despera*da*."

"La Desperada," Lauren said, in a flamenco pose. "She

tracks through the desert destroying boxes of treasure given to her by scummy, scummy men."

"I'm not ready to destroy it."

"Well, leave it on Ed's doorstep at least. We can do it tonight."

"I'm not ready for that either."

"Min."

"Leave her alone," Al said. "She's not ready."

"Well, at least tell us the most embarrassing thing in there."

"Lauren."

"Come on."

"No."

"I'll sing," she threatened.

I gave her a small sigh. Al picked up the grater again. The condom wrappers, I couldn't say. *Goofballs III. I can't stop thinking about you.* "OK, um, earrings."

"Earrings?"

"Earrings he gave me."

Al frowned. "There's nothing embarrassing about that."

"Yes there is, if you saw them."

Lauren grabbed the pad Al's mom keeps by the phone. "Draw them."

"What?"

"It'll be therapy. Draw the earrings."

"I can't draw, you know that."

"I know, that's why it'll be therapy for you and hilarious for us."

"Lauren, no."

"OK, act them out."

"What?"

"Act out the earrings, you know, like a pantomime. Or interpretative dance, yes!"

"Lauren, this isn't helping."

"Al, help me out."

Al looked at me sitting at the kitchen table. He could see I was teetering. He took a long, long sip of his lemon mint drink and then said, "I do think it would have therapeutic value."

"*Al.* Et tu?"

But Al was moving a chair out of the way to give me room. "Do you need music?" Lauren said.

"But of course," Al said. "Something dramatic. There, those Vengari concertos my dad likes. Track six."

Lauren turned it up. "Ladies and gentlemen," she said, "put your hands together for the free-dance stylings of . . . La Desperada!"

I slouched up and then, with my friends, I took my place. So you take my ticket, Ed. While the world and its crowd were cheering you, co-captain, winner of state finals, I got some applause myself.

Give this back to your sister. I'm done.

OK, one last thing. Totally forgot it was in here. I bought it sometime, when we were talking about Thanksgiving foods a million years ago. You said that stuffing was something that had to be made the same old way, with a jar of, absolutely had to be, this weird brand they hardly make, chestnuts. You are wrong, of course. Chestnuts in stuffing tastes like someone chewed up a tree branch and then French-kissed it into your mouth. I bought this to make for you on Thanksgiving. But Thanksgiving's gone now. Al and I saw all seven Griscemi films that weekend at the Carnelian, sneaking in leftover turkey sandwiches and the mashed-mint-and-lemon drinks sloshing in plastic canteens. We didn't kiss but wiped mustard off each other's mouths, is how I remember. And he just saw this. "What's that doing there?" is what he said. I told him what I'd been willing to do for you, and he wrinkled up his nose.

"Chestnuts in stuffing tastes like someone chewed up a tree branch and then French-kissed it into your mouth," he said.

"*Ew.* And—?"

"Oh yeah. And in my opinion, bluebirds are pretty."

We have a thing now, that every time he gives an opinion he has to give an extra one to make up for all his not-having-an-opinions. My end of the deal I'm holding up finally, now that I'm ready, getting rid of this stuff. "I think I read," Al is saying now, "about an appetizer thing with chestnuts, though. You wrap them up in prosciutto I think, brush them with grappa, and roast them and put a little parsley on top."

"Or maybe blue cheese," I said.

"That'd be good."

"Could we use chestnuts from a jar?"

"Sure. Wrapping something in prosciutto cancels out from a jar. Wrapping in prosciutto cancels out anything."

"Yes," I said, and so Ed, this is the thing I'm keeping. This is the thing you're not getting back. You wouldn't even know about it if I weren't telling you, its heavy heft, its goofy label, this part of us that I'm not letting out of my grasp. It makes me smile, Ed, I'm smiling.

We could try it for New Year's, Al is going to say, I know he will. We are planning an elegant supper. It's in honor, we decided after a lot of caffeinated talk talk talk about it, of nobody. So far most of the dishes are poached from *The Deep Feast of Starlings,* which we rented again and kept pausing to bicker over what it is Inge Carbonel adds, hunched over the stone oven while her blinded son plays that racing angry piece on the cello over and over, what she bastes the tiny birds with that sits bubbling on her windowsill for days and days during her brother's wake. What kind of wine it is, like we'd be able to find Greek wine even if we knew, the camera diving deep into the bottle and following it out to the wide thirsty glass. Licorice tarts, also. A soft-boiled egg with anchovy inside. Goat cheese melted on beets or maybe these chestnuts, wrapped in prosciutto, canceling out everything. Candles, real napkins. I might get him another tie. It's a plan, some of it won't work. (Sorry to hear about Annette, by the way.) But it beats bad lousy stuffing like jocks eat, Ed. Our sketches are messy, but Al and I can read it, can picture it moving forward. The New Year will make me feel, I don't know, like those huddled happys at the large wooden table, not my favorite movie but one that's got something, according to me. You wouldn't like it. Why we broke up is that you'll never see it, never a picture like that. The tremble of the soup pots, that crazy bird that pecks at the seeds in the saucer, the way the love interest sneaks up on you, several scenes before you even know for sure he's in the story. Shutting the box with a wooden shuffle, exhaling like a truck pulling to a stop, thunking it to you with a Desperada gesture. I'll feel that way soon, any sec now, friends or loved or content or whatnot. I can see it. I can see it smiling. I'm telling you, Ed, I'm telling Al now, I have a feeling.

Love, Min

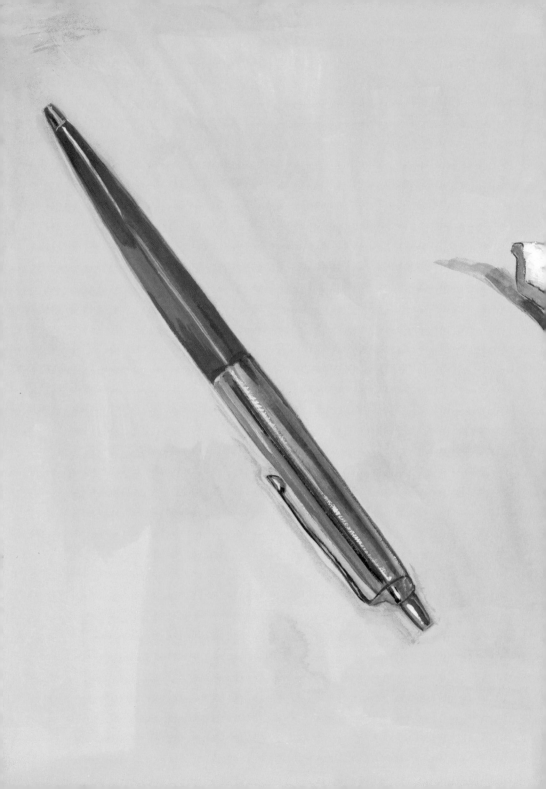